HITCHHIKING
TO
HINGNING

Family Conflicts
and Life-Altering Events

ROBERT J. RIETZ

AVL Grundisburgh LLC
Asheville, North Carolina

Author's Note

These stories relate crucial events experienced by the author or his relatives. The protagonist in *Recluse* is an exception, being a composite of individuals the author has known.

Christmas Holiday, 1945

The Visit

Marooned in Marrakesh

Recluse

Maggie

Hurricane Helene

Hitchhiking to Hingning

Hitchhiking to Hingning is a lightly edited excerpt from *Faith and Fury: An American Nun in Mao's China*, which debuts in the latter half of 2026. This historical fiction novel chronicles the persecution of Sister Marion Cordis by Chinese communists shortly after Mao came to power in 1949.

Hitchhiking to Hingning begins with Sister Marion's four-day train trip from New York to San Francisco, where she was scheduled to board a boat to China. A west coast longshoreman's strike idled California ports and, wearing her nun's habit, she hitchhiked aboard military transport aircraft across the Pacific Ocean before landing in Canton.

Contents

Christmas Holiday, 1945

Elbowing my way to the rail on the port side of the *Wilson Victory*, I shout to the GI on my right, a corporal like me. "I read in *The Stars and Stripes* that people danced in the streets when the Germans surrendered on May 8, 1945." Cupping my hands around my mouth, I holler, "Seven months ago, seems like yesterday!"

He nods before yelling back, "I saw that too, but that ain't nuttin' compared to the dance I'm gonna do when I get off this boat."

"Every man aboard wants—"

Three long and two short blasts of the ship's foghorn interrupt me as we sail by the Statue of Liberty. The

GIs on troopship

shouts of delirious families on the wharf welcoming us home the day after Christmas have grown louder since we sailed under the Verrazzano Narrows Bridge. They're visible now, even in this freezing snowstorm, and every soldier on board starts waving his cap. The cold doesn't dampen the enthusiasm that has been growing over the last seven days aboard ship.

"You got family in the crowd?" I bellow.

"Yep, wife and a son. I hope I don't crush 'em when I hug 'em. You?"

"No, my family's in Chicago, so I got a two-day train trip between me and them."

The *Wilson Victory* nestles up to Pier 88, and a metal gangplank rattles down to the dock. A Hearst Metrotone News crew films grinning GIs taking their first step onto American soil. I merge into a sea of disembarked soldiers carpeting the quay, adding to the organized chaos flooding the pier. Longshoremen unload cargo onto wagons that disappear into warehouses on my left. Trucks inch forward in every direction, honking their way through the crowd. Vulgar shouts, engine clatter, and squeaky pushcarts add to the earsplitting din.

Tearful wives reunite with husbands all around me, and grateful mothers with their sons. A wave washes over the breakwater, soaking a couple locked in a long-awaited embrace, and they break into uncontrollable laughter. I smile but I'm envious—and wet, and my shoulders sag.

A single tear crawls down my cheek, prompted by thoughts of my wife, Leola. Two years have passed since I last hugged her and said goodbye at our father's funeral. I went straight from the cemetery to the train station to a troopship to Liverpool, England. That was January 20, 1944—what a crappy day.

Leola. Five feet four inches of grace. The Mona Lisa wishes she had Leola's smile, and her soft brown eyes make me weak in the knees. With high cheekbones and wavy auburn hair down to her shoulders, she could be a model for a classical Greek statue. Her quick wit hones my sense of humor. She finished high school; I didn't. Ah, Leola.

"Soon," I say to myself, wiping away the tear.

Sleet swirls around me and I pull my wool overcoat tighter. An overpowering feeling surges through my veins. My sister is a nun in the Maryknoll Motherhouse in Ossining, a short cab ride north of the city. We've only been together once—at Dad's funeral—since the autumn of 1942, when she joined Maryknoll.

Helluva reason for a family reunion, bringing my brothers Walt, Don, and Leslie from their pre-deployment training. If I don't see Edith now, I won't see her again for who knows how long. Her October letter, which I got a week before I boarded the ship, said she'll be heading off to China soon. She'll be converting Chinese farmers to Catholicism and helping raise their families out of poverty.

Should I, or shouldn't I? I'll be AWOL if I go, but when will we have a chance to be together again? How long will my baby sister be in China? Will Maryknoll let her come home to visit? When? What will they do to me at Fort Sheridan if I go AWOL? Will they lock me up or put me on KP for week? Will I still get an honorable dis-charge? My arms fold across my chest and I frown.

On the other hand, I'd only be missing two days; it's not like I deserted during wartime. Getting discharged at Fort Sheridan is only a formality. Besides, the war is over; I need to stop behaving like a soldier and start acting like a civilian.

After hailing a yellow and black taxi, I plop into the cracked vinyl back seat and lay my garrison cap with its red and white piping next to me. "The Maryknoll Motherhouse in Ossining."

"Ossining is thirty-five miles, and it'll take about an hour and a quarter. Fare'll be around six bucks," says the taxi driver.

The Willis Avenue Bridge, an aging swing span, carries us across the Harlem River and into the Bronx, past Yankee Stadium. In this snowy off-season, The House That Ruth Built stands like a jilted bride, dressed in white and all but abandoned. Buildings sport Christmas wreaths on their doors and Christmas trees in their apartment windows. Boughs of holly hang across the top of storefront displays.

"I have severe scoliosis," says the driver, breaking the silence. "The draft board declared me 4-F."

"Eh . . . too bad, but that worked out pretty well for you." Huh. One of those guys. Somebody who stayed home and slept in a warm bed, while we risked our necks every day. How bad could his scoliosis be to keep him from being drafted?

"At least you're able to work."

"It's a living." The cabbie glances at me in the rearview mirror. "You're in uniform. Where were you assigned?"

"After basic training at Fort Lewis, I boarded a ship to troopship to Liverpool, England. We knew we were going to Normandy . . . and what was waiting for us."

"A lot of GIs sitting in the back seat have told me similar stories."

I glare at the cabbie's brown eyes in the mirror. "Those soldiers made it back home alive. A lot of 'em didn't." His eyes revert to the road.

"Uh . . . I mean . . . only a few vets talked about the war. . . . Most of their stories were about basic training, K-rations, and bad officers." An uncomfortable pause. "The trip to England. I bet coming back to New York was a lot better than going over, right?"

The cabbie's question surfaces a lesson I learned the hard way in Europe. Life is precious and I saw it snuffed out too many times.

The cab slows to a stop at a red light. Whitecaps on the Hudson River, to my left, testify to the wind and the cold. No birds are flying; the flock is huddling and fluffing themselves in leafless trees.

"Yeah, I guess. We didn't hafta worry about subs on the way back. Um, the trip over? Air cover from the States protected us for a while, and destroyers escorted our convoy the whole way, but the mid-Atlantic was crawling with U-boats." My right hand hides my lowered face, and I turn my head to the window.

The horror returns and my mind replays the night two torpedo wakes came speeding toward us. Men rushed to the rail, pointing and screaming, then raced away from where the explosions would be. The torpedoes ran straight and fast, closing the distance between us in a flash. I asked myself if this is how I was gonna die. From the explosion? Drowning? Freezing to death in the water?

I never thought a boat could turn so hard, listing at least thirty degrees. Guys hung onto anything to keep from getting thrown overboard or banging into a bulkhead. The torpedoes zipped by us, parallel to our port side, the nearest one about twenty feet away.

Luck ran out for the starboard ship in our formation. Men in the water, crying for help. Spotlights tried to find them all, but we couldn't. The captain had no choice. We had to leave, or we'd be sitting ducks for the next torpedo. Men's screams for help grew fainter that night, but not in my nightmares. What a shitty way to die.

"Let me tell you, every man on board cheered when the first squadron of British Coronados flew overhead, saluting us by dipping their wings. Every GI felt relief when he set foot on dry land, especially the fellas who got seasick every day. Uh, our company trained in Liverpool, preparing for D-Day, and came ashore on Omaha Beach on July 16, 1944. My platoon bivouacked at Barneville sur Mer our first night in Europe."

That introduction to army life continued for the next twelve months. Sleeping bags in pup tents instead of warm beds with a roof over our heads. Cold K-rations instead of hot, home-cooked meals. Trying to wash away our stink in icy rivers. Welcome to the war-time life of a US Army private.

"Returning GIs told me that Normandy after D-Day was a busy place."

"General Eisenhower worried about a German counterattack for weeks after D-Day. Men forming up on the beaches were easy targets." My upraised palms reflected our helplessness. "After D-Day, Ike ordered troops off the beach three hours after they landed. And our sergeants made damn sure we were."

"What happened next?"

"Our squad rebuilt bridges and repaired bombed-out roads, helping General Patton's Third Army carry the war into Germany."

"Sounds like there's more."

An internal dam breaks, and I offload the stress of war memories onto the anonymous listener.

"Our platoon took fire almost every day from Kraut snipers tryin' to delay our advance."

I unbutton my breast pocket and pull out a grainy photograph of four grimy soldiers leaning against a burned-out German tank, smiling and smoking cigarettes. I hand the wrinkled picture over the seat to the cabbie who glances at it.

"Some guy took this picture of my squad crossing the Rhine River a couple of weeks before VE Day. The guy on the left stepped on a landmine the next day and pieces of him went home in a body bag." A trembling sigh. "One more month . . ."

The cabbie meets my eyes in the mirror. "Sorry."

"Yeah. So were his wife and kids."

After a few minutes of awkward silence, the cabbie says, "Almost there," when a sign welcomes us to Mount Pleasant. "This is the setting for the Legend of Sleepy Hollow, or so I'm told." Snow piles up on the limbs of oak trees lining the sidewalks. Gentle hills and curves yield a few minutes later to a drunken spider web of steep Ossining streets.

The taxi enters the extensive Maryknoll campus, and I remember Edith's letters saying it's as beautiful blanketed in white as when it's covered in lush green foliage. Black squirrels frolic, jumping into snow-drifts searching for the nuts they buried in the fall. On my right, a bright red cardinal flits from limb to limb, knocking snow off a branch when it lands. Heavy snow-flakes add to the several inches already on the ground.

"Here we are."

I pay the fare and give the driver a generous holiday tip. "Merry Christmas."

"Merry Christmas, Corporal. Welcome home."

A nod, then "Thanks, and a Happy New Year."

* * *

I trudge through eight inches of powdery flakes up the slippery cement steps to the imposing double doors of the massive Maryknoll Motherhouse. A four-story stone building, its stately front stretches far down the road. The uniform rows of identical windows on the upper three floors remind me of our platoon, standing at attention, ready for inspection by some officer we'd never see again.

A nun dressed in a black habit, a cowl covering her head, answers the late-afternoon rap on the door. Her jaw drops. I stand ramrod straight on the terrace, a US Army corporal in camouflage fatigues, with white flakes blanketing me. Hands on her hips, a slight tilt of her head negates the need to ask me what business a shivering soldier might have at a convent.

"Hello, I'm Robert Baumwolle, the brother of Edith, er . . . I mean Sister Marion Cordis. My troopship arrived in New York a few hours ago, and I hoped to spend some time with her."

"Stay here and I'll fetch her." The sister shuts the door in my face, leaving me in snow up to my calves. Stomping my feet stimulates circulation, and I blow on my chilly pink hands. C'mon, hurry up and find Edith! It's freezing out here! Minutes drag by before

Sister Marion Cordis

the door reopens, enough time for my red nose to start running.

"Bob! What a wonderful surprise!" whoops Edith as I, the oldest brother, embrace her, the youngest sister, for the first time since Dad's funeral in 1944. "What are you doing here? Did the Army discharge you?"

"No, I'm AWOL. I was so close I had to come." Then a quick rationalization, "But the war is over. What can they do to me?"

"I'm not surprised, Bob. You've always had moxie. Let's not stand here in the middle of a snowstorm!" Edith steps aside and waves me in. "Come on in. Can you stay overnight? We've got so much catching up to do."

"Do I call you Edith or Sister Marion?"

"Edith when we're alone, Sister Marion when we're with the other nuns."

My sister hasn't changed since she entered the Maryknoll convent three years ago. A voluminous black habit and headpiece can't contain her bubbly personality. An ear-to-ear grin and her musical voice brings back wonderful memories of 849 Lawler Avenue in Chicago's Germantown neighborhood. Seven children and our

849 Lawler Avenue

parents lived in a thirteen-hundred-square- foot bungalow with one bathroom. A tomboy in her youth, Edith developed a thick skin to protect her from the pranks and jibes of four older brothers.

My sister leads me with a joyous bounce in her step into the stone structure, passing through the foyer into a short hallway. At the end, a chapel with pews on either side of its center aisle opens before us. Shepherds, three wise men, Mary, and Joseph share the sanctuary with baby Jesus laying in a straw-filled manger. Edith motions me to the right hallway after bowing and making the Sign of the Cross at the chapel entrance.

Maryknoll chapel

A glance to my left reveals an open courtyard, a little smaller than a football field, confirming the size of this building. Introducing me to every nun we encounter leaves shards of Maryknoll's Rule of Silence—Edith mentioned it in one of her letters—shimmering in our wake.

Maryknoll courtyard

I spend a long, satisfying day with Edith in the convent. A shared pot of tea in the Reading Room relaxes us, provoking reminisces about the old days. She's received letters from Mom with news of our brothers; Walt,

Leslie, and Don. They all survived battles in Europe and the Pacific without being wounded and are readying to board ships to bring them home. Our older sisters, Florence and Dorothy, married before Pearl Harbor and have started their families.

"The last couple of Leola's letters still have a whiff of her perfume. God, I miss her! Ooops! Sorry Edith, er, I mean Sister Marion."

"Of course you do."

"Her touch. I miss her touch on my cheek. I miss sharing a cup of coffee after breakfast, before I went to work." A deep sigh. "Tell me how you're doing."

"Bob, I've never been happier than I am now. I was born to become a Maryknoll missioner. By the way, Maryknoll calls its sisters "missioners," not "missionaries." Charles Dutton's book, "The Samaritans of Molokai," inspired me to missioner work. I wrote a book report on it in eighth grade. Ever since then, I 've wanted to spread Jesus' Gospel of Love and help families rise out of poverty."

"I remember you showing off your grade, a B plus, at our supper table. If only the rest of your grades were that good."

"Bob! Stop teasing." A sharp jab in my ribs, a bit more than a love tap, reminds me when we were kids.

"I wasn't interested in school subjects like science or mathematics. I'm an approximate person."

I must admit I enjoyed being the center of attention later as the only man, and a serviceman to boot, in the dining hall that evening. Playing this masculine role to the hilt, I stride to the first table of nuns and deliver an enthusiastic, "Good evening, ladies." The warm words are met with pained expressions and averted eyes, but I'm not deterred. Circulating among other nearby tables of future missioners, I give each one a hearty "Good evening, ladies."

Returning to Edith's table, we begin our meal with modest portions of an iceberg lettuce salad with mayonnaise, meatloaf, mashed potatoes with gravy, and green beans. The six nuns who share our table also ignore my attempts at conversation. The dining room contains around twenty tables, making the convent's population about one hundred and fifty sisters. One wall is covered with colorful posters of saints and Bible stories. The opposite wall exposes squirrels frolicking in the snowy courtyard.

Dressed in black robes with black or white headpieces, the nuns maintain complete silence, not a whisper. Everyone's refusal to respond to my casual greetings in the hallway and at dinner perplexes and frustrates me. Edith whispers one of the "house rules" in my ear after dessert, when the residents are allowed to discuss their studies. "Mother General allows us to speak only at specified times. Study, prayer, or meditation should occupy our minds when we're not talking."

Heads turn and nuns whisper when I accompany Edith into the chapel the next morning. She giggles after Mass. "You're in for a treat. Tonight after dinner, at the weekly Chapter of Faults, we'll confess our infractions of the last week. Not sins—that's for the priests—just violations of the house rules. It's a way of letting off steam after a week of study, prayer, and meditation. While it's great fun, and we all laugh, it's also a way of reminding us of our strict vow of obedience. Every nun must observe even the slightest rule without the slightest hesitation."

"A vow of obedience? Dad is laughing in his grave at that."

"Bob! Stop it! Mother General might call on you for a confession, so think about what you've done wrong in the last week. Knowing you like I do, you have a bucketful of choices."

That night, each sister receives a plate another iceberg lettuce salad and a chicken pot pie. Edith leans toward me when Mother General enters the kitchen, out of sight of our table. "Food rationing has eased but can still make dinners at the end of the month a bit skimpy. . . . During the summers, we grew lettuce, carrots, and plenty of other vegetables in our Victory Garden."

Mother General rises after the silent supper, while servers place a cherry-flavored Jello in front of each diner. "Each sister will stand and admit her shortcomings of the last week and receive a penance. The first table to reveal their despicable conduct is Sister Marion's." One by one, each of the other six sisters rises, declares a failure of her conduct, and sits.

"I ate a banana with my hands."

Quiet giggles break the silence.

"I did not tuck in my bedsheets on Thursday morning."

"I was tardy to class."

"I walked to class with one other sister."

"I didn't eat my vegetables on Wednesday."

"I sat with my legs crossed."

"Tsks" permeate the room until Mother General raps the table.

Sister Marion stands up, bows her head to conceal her smile, and says, "My mind wandered during Mass."

This Chapter of Faults is a little strange, but, in its own way, it's like life in the army. Master Sergeants taught us proper military salutes, drilled us to answer "Yes, Sir," and schooled us in other army rules in boot camp. Raw recruits learned to obey orders without thinking.

Mother General absolves each confessed sister and administers a light-hearted penance before asking Edith, "Does your brother care to unburden his soul?"

I climb out of my chair and assume the "at ease" position, clasping my hands behind my back. "I'm AWOL." Gasps fill the dining room, then silence.

"God will forgive you, but I'm not so sure about the US Army. They'll determine your penance."

"Mother General, you run a tighter outfit than the army. I'll be OK."

Edith puts her head in her hands, stifling a laugh. "How do you get away with these kinds of stunts?"

Everyone laughs, but worrisome thoughts about being AWOL creep into my consciousness as the time for me to leave Edith grows near. This visit has been worthwhile, and I'd do it again, but how will the brass react? What's gonna happen at Fort Sheridan? Will this stunt delay from me seeing Leola?

After Mass ends the next morning, Edith and I retreat to her room where we share childhood memories. I remind her when she cuddled with Dad on the carrot-colored sofa in our front room, while listening to Little Orphan Annie on the radio after supper. She reminds me when I dropped out of high school during the Depression to help Dad pay the bills. "You joined an advertising agency as a 'gofer' but learned how to sell refrigerators to Eskimos." Our time ends too soon, and I don my dress uniform.

"Bob, what are all those medals for? Are you a hero?"

"Everyone over there was a hero."

"But a Bronze Star! You have a Bronze Star! How did you get that?"

"Our unit got ambushed when we were clearing mines for General Patton's tanks. I crawled into the line of fire three times to pull wounded men to safety. A lot of guys did similar things but didn't get medals."

"What about these?" she asked, touching the ribbons.

"Those are campaign ribbons, identifying where you fought. This talk of medals and ribbons brings back thoughts of men who aren't coming home. Let's drop it."

I kiss Edith goodbye and tell her to be safe and write often.

*   *   *

Traveling from Ossining to Fort Sheridan, Illinois, involves a cab, two trains, and a bus. On the first train, I formulate a plan on how I might avoid punishment for going AWOL. The ad men at the agency constantly discussed strategy on how to sell something to a reluctant client.

"Keep 'em off balance. Tell 'em somethin' they're not expecting," explained one long-timer.

"Humor is the key. People can't say no when they're laughing," offered another.

"But you always hafta treat 'em with respect."

"Pretend like you're on the same side as they are; that you have their best interests at heart."

"Never admit you're wrong. That gives 'em an excuse to throw you out the door."

I develop my plan on the next train, anticipating reactions and objections to my spiel. I'll open with a joke, then say, "The war is over. And it's the Christmas season." Who could object to that? But doubts creep into my mind. What if the Fort Commander doesn't appreciate my sense of humor? What's my backup plan? If worst comes to worst, I'll hafta rely on my Bronze Star and other medals to emphasize our shared success in winning the war. This better work.

A cab, two trains, and a bus gets me to Fort Sheridan, Illinois the next day, late in the afternoon. A water tower, over two hundred feet tall, dominates the landscape. Two MPs check my ID at the gate and point me toward the Fort Commander's office. A sign says the individual wooden huts behind it are the Officers' Quarters.

Walking across the frozen parade ground, I pass a squat building to my left with bars on its windows—must be the stockade. A nearby sign covered with a thin layer of hoarfrost indicates the Mess Hall is another hundred yards to the left. Row after row of gray Quonset huts being used for temporary barracks lie beyond the jailhouse. Wisps of smoke escape each building's chimney. A line of barren oak trees behind these buildings marks the boundary of living quarters.

Fort Sheridan

Men in fatigues mill around the entrances, smoking cigarettes and engaging in animated conversation. I want to join them, but first I have to report to the Fort Commander and explain why I'm late. My brows furrow—I'm more than a little bit worried, but a cheerful demeanor will start me off on the right foot.

Taking a deep breath, I rap on the door of Colonel Slusser's office, march inside, drop my duffel bag, and snap off my smartest salute. "Sir! Corporal Robert

Baumwolle of the 133rd Engineer Combat Battalion Company D, reporting. Sir!"

The Fort Commander shoves his paperwork aside and eyeballs me. "Your unit checked in two days ago." His index finger draws circles in the air. "Where the hell have you been the last forty-eight hours?"

"Sir, do you want the truth or an interesting lie? Sir!"

The colonel's head jerks at my flippant attitude. Jumping to his feet, he leans over his desk with his balled fists, knuckles down, planted amid scattered documents. "Listen Corporal, I got a good mind to throw you in the stockade. Where were you?"

"Sir! My sister is doing God's work as a Maryknoll missionary. I stopped by to visit her in Ossining after my troopship dropped anchor in New York harbor. Together we thanked the Good Lord for the bad aim of German snipers. Sir!"

"No one gave you permission to get here late! You're AWOL! I could lock you up for that—for thirty days!" The colonel's roar echoes off the corrugated steel walls of the Quonset hut. "You're still in the US Army," a pounding right fist accentuates the point, "and you will," another emphatic thump sends papers seesawing to the wood floor, "obey orders!"

I grin at my commanding officer while maintaining proper military posture. "Sir, the war is over." A small snicker, "Did you hear?" followed by an ear-to-ear smirk. "We won. Sir!"

"And I can add another thirty days for insubordination!"

"Sir! Please! The war is over! What good will jailing me do? Christmas was six days ago. Have some Christmas spirit! I promised my wife that we'd celebrate New Year's together. Sir!"

"I got more important things to do than dealing with you," he says, giving me a backhanded flick of his wrist. The crewcut leader's face flushes at my insolence. "Guards!"

Two tall MPs in white helmets and conspicuous white armbands materialize. One is thin and wiry, but the shirt of the other man struggles to contain his muscular shoulders.

"Take this man to the stockade!" Colonel Slusser roars, jerking his thumb in the direction of the jailhouse. The skinny MP picks up my canvas rucksack and flings the bag at me, sending me backward. Each military policeman grabs me by an elbow to frog-march me out of the office and onto the parade grounds, bound for the lockup. I clutch my khaki bag with both hands.

"I saw combat in Europe. Did either of you serve overseas?" I ask. My right foot skims the frozen ground while the left one dangles inches from the dirt.

One MP remains silent, but the husky policeman on my left side offers his war-time experience. "I followed MacArthur in his island-hopping campaign."

Followed. The guy used a curious word to describe his war-time experience. I'll bet he never endured a single firefight.

I raise the stakes while my feet search for solid footing. "I landed in Normandy in June of 1944. The Germans surrendered a year later when they learned I'd crossed the Rhine."

The burly man tries to match my somewhat exaggerated claim. "I was stationed in New Guinea and the Philippines."

"So you experienced someone shooting at you, trying to kill you. Or were you an MP there, too?" I pause my challenge, suspecting the "armband" couldn't answer affirmatively—this time he used the word "stationed." The MP's lips press together, but he doesn't respond, though his grip on my elbow tightens.

"Hearing a bullet hit the wall next to you and feeling its impact strengthens your faith in God . . . and motivates you to improve your cover," I say. The December cold bites at my face. "Do you know what it's like to shit behind a bush? Did either of you wake to your unit being shelled at two in the morning?"

Our trio reaches the jailhouse door, and the unresponsive MP unlocks it. A few feet inside, they shove me into an empty cell in the deserted jail.

My voice hardens. "I don't see how sassing Colonel Slusser outweighs getting shot at." I stare down the Pacific Theater veteran. "How many dead men did you put in body bags to send home? Could you forget the sight of a buddy in your foxhole with half his face blown off?" Now I'm pissed. My voice lowers while the volume rises. "You always think, 'That coulda been me.' So here I am, about to be jailed for insubordination after cheating death multiple times. The fucking war is over." I shrug my shoulders and jerk out my hands, palms up.

The two MPs huddle, exchanging animated murmurs after gesturing at my regimental shoulder patch and the striking collection of service and campaign medals on my chest. "Didn't 'cha see the guy's Bronze Star?" the thin one asks. "He don't deserve this. Are we supposed to throw a Bronze Star into jail because he pissed off Colonel Slusser?"

The burly guard grits his teeth and mutters, "The Colonel said, 'Take this man to the stockade.' We've done that. If we don't fill out paperwork, there's no record of him," a nod toward me, "in here." His partner cinches his cheek and nods agreement.

The overseas veteran stomps into my cell. "Your company musters out at ten hundred tomorrow morning after breakfast, right outside." Closing the distance between us in two quick strides, he flings his beefy finger in my face, muttering, "Barracks Delta Seven is two hundred yards on the left." He pokes me in the chest. "Merry," then a harder jab, "fucking," and a final stab, "Christmas," sending me backward two steps.

The escorts abandon me standing in the open cell. A sliver of fading sunlight wedges its way between the ajar prison door and its frame, ending at my feet. I peek out the narrow doorway but decide to delay my escape until darkness overtakes the fort.

Returning to my rucksack, I sit down with my back to the wall next to the door, stretch and fold my arms, and wait. I recount the cities and towns where I've slept since July 16, 1944: Chicago, Fort Lewis, New York City,

Liverpool, Barneville sur Mer. . . . was it twenty-six or twenty-seven places? Doesn't matter.

Four thousand miles separated me from Leola no matter where I was. What am I looking forward to when we reunite? Is it a kiss that's been buried for two years, waiting to be shared? Is it her pot roast with carrots and boiled potatoes? Who am I kidding? Leola has the sweetest laugh on earth—I want to hear her laugh. I've seen Leola once, and that was at Dad's funeral, in the twenty-nine months from when I was inducted on July 24, 1943 to today, December 31, 1945. Twenty-nine long, lousy months.

A few minutes later, a series of footsteps walking toward me from my left prick my ears, but they continue without anyone noticing the crack in the jailhouse doorway.

"Wonder what they'll serve us on our last night here."

"Steak and baked potato with sour cream?"

"More likely shit on a shingle."

"Better than the K-rations we had while clearing mines."

"Quit yer bitchin'. You'll have a home-cooked meal when you get home. How far do you have—"

Mess hall! They're going to the mess hall! And it might be my company. But the MPs will be there, and they don't want to see me as much as I don't want to see them. Colonel Slusser might show up to say a few parting words to the men. I can go hungry. Missed meals weren't unusual in French foxholes; missing a couple of meals here won't hurt me.

Sweet dreams of reuniting with Leola helps me spend my idle minutes. Recalling her squeals of delight during our phone call last month, when I told her I'd be home around New Year's Eve, raises my spirits. I pull her latest letter from my duffel. "Dearest Bob," it began, "I can't wait until you walk in the door. Let's save enough money so we can move out of the apartment and buy a small house. And maybe start a family?"

I kiss the photo she included in her letter. "Soon."

What a helluva two years. Was the time wasted? Yeah, we freed Europe and prevented Hitler from invading England or the US, but I'll never use most of what the army drilled into me. Will I ever remove another land mine or shoot a rifle? Nope! Tomorrow I'll shave in a bathroom sink instead of my helmet, and I'll never eat meals out of a tin can again. Never!

Will my job at Liberty Photoengraving still be there? Will I remember how to do it? Walt worked at Liberty with me—is he home yet?

Walt fought in New Guinea and was in the Philippines when the war in the Pacific ended, three months after VE Day. Leslie battled in Okinawa, the bloodiest battle in the Pacific. My company commander said the Japs wouldn't give up and they chose suicide over surrender. Edith said both brothers were OK, but I won't believe it until I shake their hands. I can't wait until we all get home and start swapping lies.

Did I screw everything up when I went AWOL? Will Liberty give me my job back if I don't have an honorable discharge? Will the bank loan me money to buy a house? But I had to visit Edith. Now it's her turn to cross an ocean and be away from home. Yeah, I shouldn't have been such a jerk with Colonel Slusser, but I couldn't contain myself. I was so happy to be going home that the words came out without thinking.

Leola, darling, can you forgive me if my homecoming is delayed? I love you. God, how I've missed you! Rereading your letters gave me strength to survive each day. Your last letter mentioned Mom's plans for a final all-female Thanksgiving dinner last month. A mental picture of several women standing around the table with knives in their hands had me laughing for days. Which one of them carved the turkey?

Remember our honeymoon? Our eighteen-dollar jalopy overheated going up Pike's Peak and we coasted downhill until we reached a gas station, laughing all the way.

I pull her picture from my wallet and kiss it. "Soon."

Ninety long minutes later, footsteps and voices jolt me from my thoughts.

"I told you we'd have a decent meal."

"Hot dogs and beans might be your idea of a decent meal, but it sure ain't mine."

"At least we could have seconds."

"Yeah, and if you fart all night, I'll smother you with your own pillow."

I ease the door open and shut it behind me, the constant chatter drowning out its conspicuous click. Nonchalant, I sidle into the nearest cluster of men. "I wanted some beer to wash down the franks," I say to the man next to me, my breath producing vapor in the crisp nighttime air.

"That'd never happen. The brass doesn't want to deal with us getting drunk our last night in uniform. They want us out of here, and the sooner the better."

"So does every man here."

"For once the brass and the grunts agree on somethin'."

The walk to Delta Seven Barracks takes about three minutes, enough time to blend in and say hello to some men who were in my squad.

The camaraderie leads to subdued laughter while we stroll to our quarters. Once inside, my fellow GIs grumble before they settle in for the night. I wander among the bunkbeds, chitchatting, until everyone has returned to where they've slept the last two nights. After stowing my gear in an empty footlocker, I plop down on an unclaimed bunk.

"Say, Bob, I didn't notice you on the train from New York or anywhere around here the last three days," asks a teenager from the bunk on my right. "Where were you?"

My mind draws a blank on the kid's name. "I was delayed." A quick query stops this line of questioning. "When did you join and where are you headed?"

"I enlisted on my eighteenth birthday and I'm going home to Waukegan. You?"

"Downtown Chicago. Tomorrow's a big day. Let's get some shut eye." I roll over to my left, showing the inquisitive private my back. Overhead lights go out moments later.

*　*　*

After morning reveille, everyone files out for breakfast. Almost everyone. I stay behind, hiding in the latrine, crouching on a toilet in case anyone, like the MPs, enters. I emerge when the men return, and we change into full dress uniforms. This ragtag bunch transforms into a spit-and-polish unit that would pass the toughest inspection. Men tie the laces of their weathered combat boots together, never to be worn again, and some write today's date on the worn leather.

Boots begin corkscrewing through the air toward the rafters. Many pairs land with a boot on either side of an exposed joist on the first toss, but others fall back to the plywood floor. The owners fling them again and again, until every pair hangs over our heads, like Christmas ornaments. I toss mine, and they hang up on a beam. I'm not in the army anymore. The twenty-nine-month nightmare is over. Leola, here I come.

The door slams open, banging against the wall, revealing a second lieutenant with arms akimbo, silhouetted in the morning sun. The hanging boots provoke a momentary smile that distorts into a stern frown.

"ATTEN-HUT!!"

Over forty soon-to-be civilians jump to attention at the foot of our bunks.

"FALL IN!"

Hefting our gear, we march out the door, and form ranks in front of the barracks for the last time. I squeeze into the middle of the penultimate row.

"Count off."

I voice the next number when it's my turn, and the last man shouts, "Forty-six!"

The officer makes a quizzical face and glances at his paperwork before continuing. The absence of medals and campaign ribbons means he's a member of the colonel's staff, maybe a fresh graduate of Officer Candidate School. He probably discharges six or eight platoons every day.

"Every man's discharge papers have been approved by Colonel Slusser," he says, "but you ain't out of the army until he releases you, so no bullshit on the parade grounds." His index finger stabs the air. "One soldier thought he could la-di-dah into Fort Sheridan whenever he felt like it, and he's in the stockade. Anybody who goofs off will join him." The second lieutenant pauses, then, "Left face. Forward march! Hut, two, three, . . ."

The formation reaches the parade ground, and I spy Colonel Slusser twenty feet away, studying a sheet of paper with his aide-de-camp. Two familiar MPs, hands clasped behind their backs and feet shoulder width apart, flank the colonel and his assistant.

"Company, HALT!"

Forty-six pairs of feet stop in unison after ONE, TWO more strides.

"Left face!"

The maneuver concludes with heels clicking.

"Parade rest!"

Canvas bags drop to the ground, our spines stiffen, and we clasp our hands behind our backs as the Fort Commander walks to the front of the assembled troops.

My choice of position in the formation at the barracks avoided the second lieutenant questioning the presence of a new face. That choice and two marching left faces now puts me in the second row. Less than a dozen feet separate me from Colonel Slusser. My heart starts racing, threatening to explode; I'm surprised no one hears it thumping.

I shift my gaze, but not my head, to the impassive face of the burly MP and make momentary eye contact, then glance away. The MP's scowl reminds me of his hostile poke to my chest. Did he recognize me? Please buddy, don't turn me in. I'm so close to Leola now I can almost smell her perfume.

"Sir! Forty-six men of Company D of the 133rd Engineer Combat Battalion are ready for inspection. Sir!"

With a puzzled look, Colonel Slusser swivels to his aide-de-camp. Lowering their voices, they engage in a lengthy subdued conversation. The assistant's finger runs down the sheet of paper, Colonel Slusser crooks his index finger toward the second lieutenant and the MPs, motioning them to join the discussion. The aide-de-camp shrugs his shoulders.

Uh-oh. Did he say that forty-five men are being discharged? The Fort Commander folds his arms across his chest while the beefy MP begins a lengthy monologue, and the other MP nods his head. Are the MPs spilling the beans on me? Can they hear my labored breathing?

Colonel Slusser turns to face us, walks to the first man in the front row, and deliberately makes his way down the line. He pauses to shake each man's hand and study his face. The colonel continues, shakes the hand of the soldier in front of me, and peers into his eyes. Or is he looking past the man and looking at me? I dare not make eye contact.

Will he shake my hand? How can I look him in the eye? I'm supposed to be behind bars, not in line waiting to become a civilian. My brow furrows and beads of sweat appear on my forehead. How am I gonna handle this? What will he do to me? When will I hold Leola in my arms?

Colonel Slusser reaches the end of the line, then returns to the middle of the rank and pivots to face the men. "Every man in this company has served with honor. The decorations on your uniforms testify to your bravery. It's my honor, and privilege, to declare you are all civilians, the moment you walk through the gates of Fort Sheridan. The trucks outside," his left arm points toward freedom, "are waiting to take you to downtown Chicago. Enjoy celebrating New Year's Eve as civilians."

He signals to the second lieutenant, who salutes him and spins around to face the expectant veterans. "Dismissed!" yells the junior officer.

The thunderous roar eclipses the clamor from the *Wilson Victory's* rail six days earlier, and men rush to several idling "Deuce and a Halfs." I stoop to lift my duffel bag and catch Colonel Slusser glaring at me when I straighten up. He makes a subtle nod but there's not even a hint of a smile.

After returning the gesture, I rush through the gate to freedom. Freedom! I'm a civilian now! What a way to start the new year! A lengthy exhale relieves the stress of the last ten minutes and the last twenty-nine months. Leola, I'm on my way. Soon!

Stepping on a truck's bumper, I grab the handrail and hoist myself and my gear into its tarpaulin-covered bed. Fifteen other new civilians pile in after me. I settle onto a wooden bench, holding my rucksack on my lap for the bumpy and crowded forty-minute ride to downtown Chicago.

"This will be an interesting story to tell at family gatherings," I say to myself, chuckling.

My life could be a book, and I turned thirty-one just last month. Dropping out of high school in my sophomore year to work at an ad agency so Dad wouldn't lose the house during the Great Depression. Walt got me a better job at Liberty Photoengraving. Working at the same place provided opportunities for lots of laughs.

And I won't forget winning the marbles championship of the junior Knights of Columbus in 1927. The victory qualified me for the national championship in Washington DC, but my family couldn't afford to send me.

Of course, the highlight of the book would be meeting and marrying Leola. World War II intervened and I got drafted and came ashore in France after surviving a torpedo attack from a Nazi wolfpack. Too many gruesome memories from battlefields that I hope will fade with time. Going AWOL to visit Edith will never be forgotten. The book would end with us having children, maybe two beautiful daughters?

Familiar sights begin appearing on the last leg of my four-thousand-mile journey home when the truck turns onto Michigan Avenue. First, we pass by the Chicago Water Tower, followed by the Chicago Tribune Building, and then the Wrigley Building, among others. The metal Michigan Avenue drawbridge over the Chicago River shakes and rattles when our weighty truck lumbers onto it.

My eyes shut and dreams of wrapping my arms around Leola make me smile. Squealing brakes and a shout, "Everybody out!" breaks my reverie at Union

Chicago Water Tower

Station. Ex-GIs pour out of the trucks, while I search the slushy streets for a green-and-grey Chicago Checker cab amid the skyscrapers towering over me. I'm home.

"There's one." I raise my arm and yell. "Taxi!"

I howl, "Soon!"

The Visit

The landline phone on my nightstand jangled, delaying the start of my first commute to a new employer in downtown Detroit. My word-a-day calendar laid open to April 27, 1998.

"Hello?" I asked.

"Hi, Rob. It's Betty. You know those phone calls you don't wanna make, but you gotta do it?" said my sister. "This is one of them." A lengthy pause. A sniffle. "Mom died last night."

My shoulders slumped. I plopped onto the unmade bed, and my right hand dropped to my side. Lifting the receiver back up to my ear, I asked, "What! What happened?"

Susan, my wife, saw my concern and sat next to me with a puzzled look.

"Mom's dead," I whispered.

Susan's face fell, and her loving arm caressed my heaving shoulders.

I couldn't believe it. Mom was traveling with Susan and me a week ago. She was her usual funny, bubbly self. My face scrunched.

"You called me after she was admitted into the hospital, . . . a day after we dropped her off. . . . I talked to her a couple of days ago. Her voice was unrecognizable, . . . so distant . . . feeble." Stifling a sob, I said, "Mom was never sick a day in her life. How did she go downhill so fast?"

"The doctors couldn't diagnose what was wrong," Betty said. "She demanded to be released, and they sent her home yesterday. We ate dinner at her condo, to keep an eye on her because she was so faint, . . . almost like she wasn't there. Something was wrong, but . . . Now it's just you and me. We're orphans."

Shit! The fall, I thought. Two days before returning home from a memorable vacation, Mom stepped off a curb without knowing it. Her head bounced on the pavement, scraping her cheek and forehead. Was that the reason for her quick deterioration? But she was her typical irrepressible self the next two days—joking, laughing, and raging about politics. Should I have been paying more attention to this seventy-eight-year-old woman?

"Rob? Are you still there?"

"Yeah, I was just thinkin'. I'll call work and tell 'em what happened. We'll pack and leave in about an hour."

"OK. See you then. I hafta make more calls. Make the necessary arrangements. Huh. This'll be the last thing I'll hafta do for Mom or Dad. I've had that responsibility for eleven years, ever since they moved near Tom and me."

"OK. We should be in Raleigh around eight o'clock tonight."

"Do you mind sleeping at Mom's? We don't have an extra bedroom."

"Yeah, we can do that. Bye."

* * *

Memories and self-recriminations surfaced during the grim marathon drive to Raleigh. I had abdicated parental oversight to Betty and enjoyed Mom and Dad's attention and affection when I "parachuted in" twice a year. Betty did the difficult day-to-day tasks of driving them to doctors' appointments, grocery shopping, and taking them to lunch, all with her two young kids in tow. This injustice was just the next chapter after our childhood, when we fought like cats and dogs.

Dad had suffered a near-fatal heart attack in 1977 when my parents lived in Chicago. They agreed the brutal winter was too difficult for Dad and decided to move near one of their children. Susan and I had settled about thirty miles outside Detroit in 1975, where the winters were as debilitating as Chicago's. Migrating to North Carolina, around the Raleigh area, made more sense because Betty and Tom had settled in a suburb north of the Research Triangle several years earlier.

Remembering fierce Chicago winters reawakened my memory of the "broken window affair." Mom worked while Betty and I attended grammar school; I was in sixth grade, and Betty was in third. New carpeting was an extravagant Christmas present from our parents to the family, installed in our parlor and dining room, lofty titles the rooms didn't deserve. Dad had told us, "Go in the back door when you get home from school and take off your boots on the back porch. Don't step on the carpet with snowy boots."

I walked faster than Betty and always got home before she did. Being the dutiful son, I unlocked the back door, unbuckled and removed my galoshes, and entered the parlor in my stockinged feet. A few minutes later, Betty rang the front doorbell.

"Let me in! I'm cold!"

"Dad said to go in the back door."

Betty began beating on the door, and my denials got louder.

"Please! It's freezing out here!"

Playing the role of the obedient son, I was enforcing Dad's directive. Rules were rules. I went in the back door, and so could Betty. No exceptions. The volume of my refusals increased again, as did her pounding on the front door and the side window.

Until the glass broke and tumbled over the windowsill onto the snow-covered porch. The shattered glass brought me back to earth. Mouth agape, I opened the front door, and Betty removed her boots on the welcome mat before she walked in.

In retrospect, was I wrong? Of course. Betty was at a disadvantage, and I enjoyed her discomfort. I was being a jerk. Was she wrong? Yep, but not nearly as much as me.

* * *

The drive from a northern Detroit suburb to Betty's house was a blur. Michigan soon turned into Ohio, and five hours and a driver-switch later, a Depression-era bridge over the Ohio River welcomed us to West Virginia. "Almost Heaven," the sign boasted. Mom and Dad's new address for eternity.

Mom was a phenomenal baker. Smelling fresh-baked bread when I walked into the house after grade school was a preview of heaven on earth. My reward for waiting for the loaf to cool was a slice off the crusted end, with creamy butter melting through it. Trying to swipe a cookie fresh from the oven often provoked a rebuke. Her voice would pierce the tempting aroma. "Rob, don't touch 'em. Let 'em cool."

Dark clouds began following us when we crossed into Virginia, where we switched drivers again. A chill fell over me when I replayed my conversation with Betty about sleeping in Mom's condo. My parents had maintained separate bedrooms in Chicago due to Dad's snoring, an arrangement they continued in the Raleigh condo. They purchased twin beds, one for each bedroom, as part of their move to the Sunbelt. I turned to Susan, my hand on the key in the ignition.

"Do you mind sleeping in Mom's room?"

"Sure."

I had slept in Dad's bed on my previous visits and had felt uneasy in it at first, after he passed, but became accustomed to it over the years. The thought of sleeping in the bed where Mom had just spent her last night on earth was too much, too soon. Did it still have her "Mom" smell?

Rain began pelting the windshield when we crossed into North Carolina, a few miles west of Mount Airy, the fictional town of Mayberry in *The Andy Griffith Show*. An evening staple in our Chicago parlor in the early 1960s, each episode presented life lessons for Andy and Opie. Aunt Bea prepared their meals because Opie's mother was dead. Ron Howard's character spent much time in the kitchen, learning about life from Aunt Bea while she cooked.

Likewise, Mom and I often shared two pieces of pickled herring on crackers while she was preparing dinner. I always thought I was getting a treat. In fact, the oily appetizer was a bribe for her admission into my world; what my day was like, what was happening in my life. It was our time together. Everyone in our family knew I was her favorite, and Betty was Daddy's little girl, born after her two older brothers. Were their preferences the root cause of the lifelong discord between Betty and me?

Betty being with Mom when she died would be another example of my selfishness, compared to Betty's everyday attention to our parents. I wasn't there; she was. In my heart, I knew it wouldn't have been possible for me to be by her side—it was too sudden. I'll have to carry that burden, not being there to say goodbye and thank you for being my mother, for the rest of my life.

During the six years after Dad died, Mom lived with Susan and me for a month every summer, a relief from Raleigh's oppressive summer heat and humidity. Mom spent most of every day with my kids; walking in the neighborhood, telling stories of her childhood, and playing board games. She baked chocolate chip cookies with our kids during her stay and would give my oldest daughter a familiar rebuke. "Barb, don't touch 'em. Let 'em cool." Good times, gone forever.

Susan and I pulled into Betty's driveway at 7:35 pm and trudged up to her front porch. She opened the door before I rang the doorbell, and we hugged, longer and more earnest than we had in years. Almost my height and slender compared to my robust frame, Betty's light brown hair framed her red and puffy eyes. Inside, we exchanged meaningless pleasantries on the front room sofa, both of us avoiding opening past wounds.

"Susan and I shared driving, so the ride down wasn't too bad."

"How long did it take?"

"I dunno, ten or eleven hours."

"That's about what Tom thought it would take."

"Are your kids still doing great in school?" I asked.

"Yes, they both got straight A's on their last report card. What about your kids? Are they coming?"

"My kids are fine. They're flying down tomorrow afternoon. Susan will pick them up at the airport."

That was it, I thought. That's what was bothering me. Your kids had some benefits that mine didn't. They got to visit their grandparents any time they wanted. Your kids have memories that mine will never have. And spending time with Mom and Dad wasn't all work. Jealousy sometimes bubbled inside me when I got letters with photos tucked inside, of laughing faces at birthdays, soccer games, and school plays.

Measuring my words, I asked, "How are you doing?"

"It's been hard. Yesterday she was here, and today she's gone. I've got a lot of hard work the next few days."

I corrected Betty, saying, "Both," emphasizing the word, "of us have a lot of hard work to do." Betty and I needed to be a cohesive team to manage the next few days. This wasn't the right time to stir up past issues, but I couldn't let her have an emotional advantage. A broad outline of the work ahead of us followed, starting the next morning at the funeral home. The Rietz family always avoided confrontation, so I didn't mention Mom's accident. The guilt overwhelmed me, and admitting my negligence might have been the cause of her death could have triggered an uproar.

Susan and I followed Betty and Tom to Mom and Dad's development, about five minutes away. Purple flowering dogwoods greeted us at the subdivision's entrance, a stark contrast to the building's faded grey beadboard on its outside walls. Walking through the parking lot, I remembered my usual welcome when I traveled to my parents' North Carolina home, "Hi Rob, c'mon in!" Dad would greet me at the door, "It's good to see ya! How was your flight?"

Betty unlocked the deserted first-floor unit, and the four of us walked into a silent apartment. I'd visited many times since they moved to the Raleigh area in 1978. The condo's ubiquitous design matched eighty percent of two-bedroom 850-square-foot floor plans across America. The modest foyer forked with a galley kitchen on the right, while two more steps led to a pedestrian living room. A sliding glass door on the far wall provided a view of a neighboring subdivision, and a television and frayed couch faced each other on opposite mint-green walls.

The laminated cabinet under the TV sported a potted begonia, wilted from a week without water. A full bathroom in the hallway on the left separated the two bedrooms. Betty clarified that Mom's room was on the left; Dad's was on the right.

"Yeah, I know, but why do you keep calling it Dad's room?" After all, he passed eight years ago.

"Because it reminds me of him, that's why. And the other one will still be Mom's room, until I sell this place."

Another pointed reminder that Betty would take on yet another assignment by herself after Susan and I went home.

Tchotchkes on end tables, a glass coffee table, and a cabinet triggered fond memories. I picked up a framed photo of my graduation from Michigan State University. Mom and Dad were so proud; I was the first one in our family to graduate from college. But our parents paying out-of-state tuition created another controversy between Betty and me that has lasted fifty years. Why couldn't I have attended an Illinois university, which would have been a lot cheaper?

Turning the frame over, a red dot, about the size of a dime, caught my eye. Mom had told us she placed colored stickers on the bottom of her belongings, identifying the intended recipient after her death. My color was red, Betty's was blue, and Mom wrote the grandkids' initials on white stickers. I took a painting off the wall above the couch and checked its back, where it bore a blue dot.

"I thought I was gonna get the painting of the Chicago lakefront in the '50s," I said.

"I told Mom I really liked it and showed her where I would hang it in our family room."

"But she promised it to me."

"She changed her mind."

Susan reached for my right hand and squeezed it, her signal to drop the conversation. She was right. The painting meant more to Betty than to me. Besides, maybe it was part of the price for being our parents' caregiver for all those years. Sighing, I replaced the commonplace art on the wall.

"OK, I'll see you at eight in the morning," I said.

"See you then."

Susan and I bade each other good night with a chaste kiss, and we retired to our assigned bedrooms.

Susan took Mom's room, where Fred, my older brother, had withered from cancer and passed away nine years earlier. A lifetime heavy smoker, Fred had a lung removed in his forties. Steady work eluded him after the operation, living alone in Maryland. I paid his for a few months when the cancer metastasized, confining him to his apartment. He became unable to care for himself, and Mom drove to Maryland and brought him to live his last few weeks with her and Dad.

Betty and Fred had developed a close relationship for reasons I never understood, and Fred's death devastated her. I had traveled to Raleigh to say goodbye to my brother two weeks before he died. She was at his side his last few days and when he passed, comforting him. I was six hundred miles away and parachuted in for his funeral.

In Dad's bedroom, several hand-drawn sketches of life aboard his troopship crossing the Pacific, arrayed above the headboard, prompted my first smile of the day. Dad was proud of his service during World War II, in New Guinea, Morotai, and the Philippines, though he was reluctant to talk about it. A picture of him in uniform (a blue dot on the back) stood out among the photos of his wedding, three children, and eight grandchildren arranged on his dresser.

A familiar photograph caught my attention. A six-year-old boy grinned at me. He wore fuzzy chaps while sitting on a tired palomino in front of our house in Chicago. When did he grow up and have children of his own? A reassuring red sticker appeared when I flipped it over.

An intense urge awakened me that night. My fiftieth birthday would arrive in three months, and I had accepted my prostate as a personal alarm clock—three in the morning was the typical time it woke me. Several unsweetened iced teas on the road trip and a soda on the sofa at Betty's house exacerbated my bladder issue. After throwing off the covers, I clambered out of bed and into the hallway.

I didn't make it far. A short, plump woman stood in the narrow hallway, blocking the path to the toilet. I heard, "It will be OK, Rob." I felt the pressure of her arms on my shoulders and back, and inhaled the smell of her hair, her head resting against my neck.

I nodded. "I know," and she began relaxing her embrace. A couple more heartbeats, and she released me, then stepped backward into the blackness. I hurried into the bathroom and slipped into the inky corridor after I finished. I peered into the darkness to my right and to my left. Empty. Taking three steps to my right, I peeked at Susan in Mom's bed, asleep, breathing deeply. I was alone, an orphan.

Marooned in Marrakesh

My wife, Maureen, and I flew to Morocco to visit Michael, our only son, on Friday, August 31. Mike had completed half of his two-year Peace Corps commitment, serving near Ait Tamlil, a remote village high in the Atlas Mountains. We spotted a grinning Mike—at six feet six inches, he stood out in the crowd— waving at us from the other side of Immigration and Customs in the Casablanca airport. He welcomed us to Morocco with a chilled bottle of water in each hand, after Maureen eventually released him. She smiled up at her baby boy, saying, "I've missed you so much!" and hugged him again for good measure.

"The heat in Morocco sucks the moisture out of your body," he said. "Get used to carrying one of these around with you all the time you're here."

One step out of the air-conditioned airport, we understood his advice. After hauling our luggage to the cab stand, sweat started running down my neck and I felt my armpits getting wet. Four large gulps of water later, the three of us piled into a taxi. Guttural barks and chirps from the front seat stunned Maureen and me. Mike was speaking to the driver in Berber, a language somewhat related to Arabic. Driver and passenger had no difficulty communicating, given their gestures and laughter.

After a couple of days sightseeing in Casablanca, we boarded the Marrakesh Express. Mike brought me back to earth after I started humming the catchy Crosby, Stills, and Nash song. "Yes, that's the name of this train. I've ridden it several times, but believe me, it's no express."

A cab took us from the Marrakesh station to our rented condominium on the outskirts of the city. While unpacking, we noticed a sign on the phone, alongside its number, stating it accepted incoming calls but blocked outgoing ones.

A nearby internet café was our only connection to the outside world. An email to our daughters confirmed our arrival in Marrakesh and included the condo's phone number, noting its limited utility. From there, we set out to do our grocery shopping for the week at a store laid out much like those in the US. The earthy scent of cumin permeated the air. We entered the checkout lane with a pushcart loaded to capacity.

The person behind us made a harsh comment to his friend, and Mike turned and retorted with some terse words in Berber. I couldn't understand what either one said, but I didn't need a translation. The angry man was pointing at our shopping cart and then at other carts. He was comparing the Americans' overflowing cart to those of neighborhood Moroccans, which were filled much more modestly.

We visited Mike's posting three miles outside Ait Tamlil, a four-hour trip in a van maneuvering on narrow switchbacks in the Tizi n'Tichka Pass through the Atlas Mountains. Palm trees became scarcer before disappearing. Olive trees and scrub brush replaced them, better able to coerce water and nutrients from the cracked clay soil. Scrawny mountain goats grazed on any available vegetation, and some of them climbed the olive trees to munch on the tasty fruit. Mike assured us the ride was routine, but he pointed at a wrecked bus in a valley a couple of hundred feet below us.

"It happens," he said, shrugging his shoulders. "I jumped off a flatbed truck in May; it started swaying in the mud after a heavy rainstorm. The driver regained control in another hundred feet or so, and I climbed back on."

Mike relieved our boredom and distracted our concerns during the journey by describing his posting. Home was a primitive settlement without running water or a sewage system, and with sporadic electricity in the sole marketplace shop. Residents restricted the community's well-water to irrigating fields and drinking water for their domesticated livestock. Water for cooking and personal hygiene came from another well lying across a deep gorge, requiring a two-mile detour on flat land. Mike's morning routine, before the blistering afternoon heat, began with walking to the distant well with two five-gallon jerricans, each weighing forty-two pounds on the return trip. He told us that sometimes he made the trip twice during the day with one jerrican, depending on if Muhammad, his best friend in the hamlet, would walk with him later.

Muhammad greeted us when we stepped out of the van. "Hamoo," he said, wrapping his arms around Mike. "Assalamu alaikum."

"It's how Muslims say 'hello,'" Mike said. "It means 'peace be upon you.'"

"He called you 'Hamoo,'" I said. "Is that the Berber translation for Michael?"

"They named me "Hamoo" because of my height and shaggy hair and beard. Hamoo is a Berber spirit, tall and unkempt, who guards against intruders. Muhammad gave me the name the first time I wore my *djellaba*, the men's traditional Berber robe."

Muhammad had prepared a delicious tagine stew for lunch, washed down with cups and cups of traditional Moroccan mint tea. Mike had warned us not to eat with our left hand, considered dirty in Muslim countries, and not to take food from another person's quadrant of the tagine. Moroccans considered "poaching" as rude as an American stabbing a shrimp from their partner's salad without asking. It's that offensive. Sitting cross-legged on the floor, my left-handed wife complied admirably as we enjoyed an unforgettable meal of goat, carrots, eggplant, potatoes, and Moroccan herbs.

Maureen gasped and I cringed when we accompanied Mike into his deplorable living arrangement. My son lived in an eight-by-ten-foot windowless hovel with a dirt floor, smaller than his bedroom at home. A rickety table opposite his rope bed held a propane-powered burner for cooking, a cobalt blue basin for washing, and ceramic plates and bowls for eating. No one in this community used silverware. I reached to nab a spider above Mike's bed, but he stopped me.

"Dad, leave him alone. He's my entertainment at night, before I go to sleep."

Facing another lengthy ride back to Marrakesh, we relieved ourselves in the common privy, a ditch about a hundred yards downhill from the hamlet's huts.

* * *

The next afternoon, Mike took us to the Jemaa el-Fna, a vast open square, large enough to swallow a couple of football fields. An occasional acrobat, musician, or organ grinder with a dancing monkey prevented the plaza from being vacant.

"My cousin defanged the snake. It will dance for you. Take picture," insisted the snake charmer in broken English, so I paid him for the show. He took the cover

Jemaa el-Fna

off the wicker basket and shook the container. A cobra rose from its home and flared its hood, swaying with its owner while he played the flute. My telephoto lens enabled me to take the picture from a safe distance.

Evening transformed the Jemaa el-Fna into a mass of humanity. A labyrinth of booths crammed with spices, leather goods, caftans, and other handmade goods crammed the marketplace. Grills offered fresh lamb and vegetable kabobs, the aroma too tempting to decline, so we didn't. A flavorful and exotic experience. Magicians, minstrels, henna tattoo artists, and fortune tellers replaced the plaza's previous inhabitants. Music emanating from curious instruments permeated the bazaar's atmosphere. Foreign sights, smells, and sounds overwhelmed our senses.

"How often does this happen?" I asked Mike. "Going from almost deserted to crowds of thousands."

"Every night, Dad. This happens every night."

* * *

The past few days had tired us out, and we decided Tuesday morning to cancel the day's sightseeing. We spent the day lounging by the pool, drinking lots of water, and jumping in the pool to cool off. In the late afternoon, a leisurely stroll brought us back to the condo to begin cooking dinner. After searching in vain for an English-speaking channel on TV, we settled on the Moroccan version of CNN.

The black-and-white television showed a close-up of a smoking skyscraper, but we couldn't identify the building or guess its location from the clear sky in the background. Why did the station keep showing the fuzzy video feed of this building? Replay after replay. The three of us couldn't figure out what we were seeing. Arabic characters streamed across the bottom of the screen.

"Mike, can you read the crawl?"

"I can speak Berber and a little Arabic, but I can't read it."

"Do you understand what they are saying?"

"No. They're speaking a polished Arabic, using words I don't know."

We changed channels until we found a French station, but my college French was hopelessly inadequate for reading the crawl. Until the words "États-Unis," "New York," and "Pentagone" accompanied film of the airliner exploding into the skyscraper, the skyscraper collapsing, and then an unmistakable image of the Pentagon on fire.

Something was horribly wrong.

We stood in front of the TV, too stunned to move. More replays of the horror. We couldn't deny what we were watching.

"The Pentagon must've been hit too," I said. "But where is the building? What city?" I shook my head in disbelief. "All they're showing us is the building, clear sky, and the plane."

We continued flipping from one station to the next, looking for more information and gained the barest understanding of what had happened. After a couple of hours, we got a fuller account of the strikes when we stumbled across an English-language program broadcast from Berlin. Many questions remained unanswered when the program reverted to Arabic after a few minutes.

I choked out what we had learned. "Somebody . . . who? . . . flew airplanes into the World Trade Center buildings and the Pentagon. And why, for God's sake!"

"Are we at war?" asked Maureen.

"Who knows?" said Mike.

Sitting in our condo in Marrakesh, we searched for answers to our questions about the massacre. How many Americans died? Who did it? Why did they kill innocent people? Are there other attacks across the US? On a more personal level, I also thought of the Americans trapped in Iran when militants captured the US Embassy in 1979. Would we be arrested at the airport when we tried to leave Morocco and be held hostage?

Maureen paced the tile floor, sobbing and quietly chanting, "Why?" as if she were in a trance. Her swollen red eyes downcast, she tried to busy herself in the kitchen, to no avail. She shuffled into our bedroom and closed the door, and her wailing confirmed our helplessness. I was supposed to be "the rock," a strong man to protect our family from all harm, but my family could be in danger. How much danger I couldn't imagine. I made several trips to the box of Kleenex we had bought in the market. We'd need to buy another box, maybe two.

Not being able to call anyone frustrated us. Isolated in a foreign country, unable to speak the language, we were defenseless. The phone's ringer shattered the silence, and the caller spoke English, asking for Mike.

"Hello? This is Michael Rietz."

A Peace Corps official identified himself and said, "Volunteers are meeting at our safe house in the city. You know the building. It's where Peace Corps members go to get away and clear their heads. Leave now."

"I'm here with my parents, in an apartment. I can't leave them."

"'I'll be giving the volunteers an up-to-date briefing at eleven o'clock."

"OK. Goodbye."

Mike hung up the phone and turned to me.

"Dad, give me a hundred dollars so I can buy a radio that can receive the Voice of America or the BBC. I'll go to the safe house, learn what's happening, and then I'll be back."

After giving Mike five twenty-dollar bills, I watched my only son walk out the door, not knowing what he would face outside or if he'd return. Maureen and I stayed put—glued to a television we couldn't under-stand. We collapsed on the couch.

Mike joined the Peace Corps a week after graduating from Michigan State University—over my strenuous objections. The possibility of an accident occurring far from a hospital, lack of quality medical care, cultural conflicts, and other arguments fell on deaf ears. The adult son had inherited his father's stubbornness; he was going. Should I have been more forceful? Would it have made a difference? After all, he was a grown man. Why are the hands on the clock moving in slow motion?

Mike walked in the door six agonizing hours later with a fuller story of what had happened. We had been monitoring the Berlin station, which broadcast in English for thirty minutes every two hours, and updated its news reports bit by tiny bit. Mike's recounting of the Peace Corps members' meeting agreed with what we had learned from the television. Turning on the radio, we found the Voice of America, which confirmed the details Mike had just told us.

Terrorists had attacked America.

The three of us kept asking each other who hated the United States so much that they would conceive and commit such a heinous crime? Was their unbridled envy at our freedoms what aroused their hatred? We speculated that a more mundane reason—jealousy of our standard of living—might have motivated the hijackers. Our full shopping cart and the incident in the checkout lane came to mind.

Sleep did not come easy that night.

*   *   *

The phone rang the next morning, September 12, and we rushed to answer it.

"Dad? Are you OK? Is Mike with you?" asked Laura, our daughter.

"Yeah, we're OK for now. Mike came back from a Peace Corps safe house last night, where their leader talked to them. But what's happening? Who did this? And why?"

"I've been calling you for hours and couldn't get through. The international phone lines are so clogged, I couldn't even get a dial tone. Leave now! Come home!" Laura begged us through her sobs. "You're not safe there!"

"But the US has grounded all aircraft. We couldn't get home if we tried."

"Fly to Canada. They're accepting incoming flights."

"Mike said we're safe here, as long as we keep a low profile. We're not scheduled to leave until Friday. We'll come home then, if flights are allowed in."

"No! I got through to Carl Levin, Michigan's US senator. He didn't know when flights would resume to America, but he told me you should go somewhere in Europe as soon as possible."

The three of us had huddled around the telephone earpiece, then Mike jumped back.

"No! You guys gotta stay. They're not here, so they don't know the situation as well as I do. You're safe here." Mike had befriended many Moroccans and couldn't believe we were in danger from them. He was adamant that we stay. The sin of the father's stubbornness had been visited on the son.

"Laura, Mom and I'll talk about it with Mike. We can't call you, so give us a call tomorrow."

"Dad! No! You gotta leave! Now!"

"Laura, we can't leave right now. It's impossible."

"No, Dad, it's not! Pack up tonight and get to the Marrakesh airport. I checked. It has lots of flights to Europe. There's even a flight to Amsterdam. You could wait there until flights are allowed back into the US."

"No!" Mike interjected. "They're safe here. Besides, the terrorists could be planning on hijacking flights into Europe. They know Americans will be flooding the European airports. Let's see what happens the next couple of days."

I told my adult children to stop arguing. Mike was right; the next two days would tell us all we need to know about whether we were safe in Marrakesh or if we should try to fly out. And Mike and the other Peace Corps volunteers provided good on-the-ground intelligence that people in the States didn't have.

"Dad, please!"

"Laura, we're gonna stay put. We love you."

A wail on the other end preceded a choking "I love you."

"I love you too." A sharp inhale held back some of my tears. "We'll see you in a few days. Goodbye."

Click.

A heartbreaking call, tearing us between two of our children. The discordant conversation ended with us not knowing when, or if, we would hear from her again. At least we would see her when we returned to the States. We weren't sure whether that was true for Mike.

The telephone rang forty minutes later.

"Michael Rietz?"

I handed the phone to him.

"Yes, this is Mike Rietz."

"The agency is considering evacuating the entire Peace Corps, about one hundred and thirty of you, to Europe. All Peace Corps volunteers are urged to stay in close touch."

"OK, but our telephone doesn't allow outgoing calls, even if it's local." Mike paused before asking, "I'm staying with my parents in an apartment. Is it safe for us to leave it?"

"We don't encourage going out, but you should stay away from the US Embassy and be inconspicuous. Avoid demonstrations. Don't do anything to identify yourselves as Americans. Speak as little as possible to locals."

"OK. Got it. Goodbye."

Mike summarized the brief conversation for us. Skeptical, I wondered how an obviously American family with a six-foot-six adult male could be inconspicuous.

We ventured out to the internet café, whose terminals now all featured screensavers depicting the airliners crashing into the Twin Towers. Mike changed the screen savers on the three terminals we rented—precipitating a heated exchange in Berber between Mike and three irate Moroccan toughs. We were not being inconspicuous.

The trio advanced toward Mike in a semi-circle and the biggest teen spat out another derisive comment. I understood its meaning. Mike took a step forward, towering eight inches above the loudmouth but didn't reply. My son's clenched fists hung at his side. Fear for our safety increased, and I chose which teenager I'd fight if they tried to gang up on Mike. I hadn't been in a fistfight since the eighth grade, almost forty years ago. Would a fat fifty-two-year-old man be any good in a free-for-all?

I stepped forward, next to Mike; he pushed me backward. My mouth went dry and my heartbeat sky-rocketed. No way I was going to let these punks beat the crap out of my son. No way! I moved back next to Mike. Did any of them have a knife? I glanced at their hands. They were empty. Good. The leader pointed at Mike and then laughed at me. He hurled a final insult before waving his right arm over his head and directing the group toward the café exit.

Relief preceded a multitude of typos when I logged onto my email and sent a message to our daughters, confirming we were still safe.

My employer had offices in one of the World Trade Center towers, but I couldn't remember which tower—there were several of them. Were any of my colleagues killed when the Twin Towers collapsed? Who could tell me? I couldn't access my work email from an unsecured computer. Then I remembered someone from our Detroit office with a unique surname. Using the format of our work email addresses, I guessed at his work email address and asked whether any of our New York colleagues had been killed.

In 2001, there was no instant messaging or texting, and with a six-hour time difference, email responses chewed up the better part of a day. I hit Send, and a realization hit me. There would be no way to tell whether anyone had received my messages until the next day. Being alone, in a hostile country, with little means of communication, deepened my apprehension.

Back on the city streets, the searing afternoon heat prompted us to drain our last bottles of water. A fan blowing cool air at a convenience store's entrance proved impossible to resist. After placing a six-pack of water from the cooler next to the cash register, I reached for my wallet.

"Assalamu alaikum," said the genial proprietor, with a modest bow.

I returned his greeting, "Assalamu alaikum," wishing him peace that I didn't have.

"This is not who we are," he said in impeccable English. "They have shamed our religion and our country. Can you find it in your heart to forgive us?"

My head jerked up and stared into his earnest brown eyes. Our gaze lasted for several seconds—one human being to another. After what seemed like several minutes, I blinked and nodded my head.

"Yes. Assalamu alaikum," I said, pulling some wrinkled Moroccan currency from my wallet.

The shopkeeper shook his head and held up his hands in protest.

"My gift to you."

We trudged back to the condo in the blistering heat, grateful for the man's kind gesture. I tried to reconcile the charity of Mike's friend, Muhammad, and the generous merchant, with the hostility in the supermarket and the teenagers at the internet café. And the latest report identified the terrorists as Arabs, some of them from Morocco. The vision of the crumbling Twin Towers wouldn't leave my mind. Three thousand dead

Americans. But the sincerity of Muhammad and the storekeeper couldn't be denied.

* * *

The next day, September 13, was a blur. We went to the internet café in the morning for the latest news, but reports on the web continued to be sketchy and inconsistent. My empty inbox meant my Detroit coworker hadn't replied. Why weren't people responding to my desperate pleas for accurate information? In retrospect, I now understand the people at home were busy processing their own grief and shock and weren't monitoring email. We remained isolated in a foreign, hostile country.

But the top story sent my spirits soaring—the airline embargo would be lifted on Friday, September 14. Our scheduled return flight from Amsterdam would be among the first wave of airliners allowed across the Atlantic. Once again, we faced saying goodbye to our son, who would not discuss coming back to the United States with us, uncertain whether we would see him again.

"Dad, I'm going back to Ait Tamlil. People there don't care I'm an American. They care about their next meal. I'm helping them build a bridge so the other well will be a lot closer. It'll save them an hour a day. I'll be OK."

"Mike! That's not the point! Some people, Arabs, like the hijackers, hate Americans! They'll do anything to kill Americans! One of them could walk up to you on the street and stab you!"

"That's not gonna happen."

"But it could! Your Mom and I couldn't live with it, knowing you died alone, five thousand miles from home."

Dad! You're being dramatic. I'll be careful where I go. I'll be OK."

We hugged. Weeping, I pleaded, "Mike, please be safe. Keep in touch. Tell us everywhere you go. I love you. Please be safe."

Would we ever see Michael again? The question was never asked aloud, but I kept asking myself. Memories of Mike taking his first steps, reading him bedtime stories, playing basketball, his first girlfriend, high school graduation. His hovel in the Atlas Mountains. Would memories be all we have of him?

*　*　*

Maureen and I hailed a taxi to the train station, waving goodbye to Mike. Tears ran down our cheeks, and we clutched each other. The conductor gave our puffy, bloodshot eyes a quizzical glance before welcoming us aboard the Marrakesh Express. Detraining in Casablanca, we hailed a taxi to take us to the airport, where we loaded our carry-on bags onto the screening conveyor. Despite the events of the week, no one was monitoring the X-ray machine when our luggage passed through it. Crazy, I thought. Nothing this last week made sense.

We landed in Amsterdam the night before our scheduled departure to the United States. None of the local hotels had an opening, so we stayed overnight in a youth hostel. Isolated again, we lacked any means of communication and didn't know what we would face in the morning. I listened to Maureen toss and turn and sigh all night in the bunk bed below me.

The next morning, September 14, we arrived at the Amsterdam airport four hours early in case any problems arose going through security. A madhouse awaited us. People shouted and shoved their way to their gates, and hippies tried to discreetly dispose of contraband. Nearby policemen displayed no interest in hallucinogenic drugs and told them not to bother getting rid of their hash stash.

Yet my wife's eyelash curler aroused the suspicion of the X-ray screener, so she showed him how it worked.

Not satisfied with her demonstration, a suspicious offi-cial searched our carry-on bags item by item, despite them having gone through the X-ray scanner moments earlier.

This display of caution didn't prepare us for the next step in the security process. A stern policeman with a holstered sidearm interrogated every passenger. When our turn came, the Moroccan stamp in our passports aroused his suspicion, and he wanted to know why we'd been there. We explained our son was a Peace Corps volunteer in Morocco. The armed policeman quizzed us where Mike was posted, why we'd chosen this exact time to travel, had we met anyone else in Morocco, and what were we bringing back. Every time we gave him an answer, it led to another question.

And then he started over, from the beginning, veri-fying the consistency of our answers. When he finished, we tried to walk past him, but he held out his arm and barked, "Stop!"

What did we say wrong? My father always said that liars needed a good memory, but I wouldn't need one if I told truth. And we did.

The policeman asked the same questions a third time, but in a random order, again listening for any variation in our responses. After twenty long minutes, he ushered us into a holding area, and the door locked behind us. The reinforced door opened only to let other passengers into, not out of, the secure room. Isolated and cut off again.

Boarding the plane took forever. One soldier blocked the line of people in the jetway about twenty feet from the airliner, releasing one person at a time. Two other soldiers, one with a rifle, stood in the plane's boarding door. The second soldier admitted each passenger after comparing their boarding pass and passport. We settled into our seats, the cabin's silence broken by the sound of overhead bins being opened and closed.

The ashen flight crew and attendants maintained a professional demeanor with forced smiles. Only when the plane began taxiing did people start talking to others seated around them. Many had been stranded for days and related stories of trying to find somewhere to stay without a reservation and similar travel problems. The aircraft engines revved for takeoff, and cries of relief flowed freely throughout the cabin when the wheels left the runway.

The pilot came on the intercom once we climbed to ten thousand feet. "Ladies and gentlemen, you may not walk around the cabin. You must remain in your seats with your seatbelt fastened for the duration of the flight. Ring the call button for a flight attendant if you need to use the restroom. They will accompany you to the restroom and escort you back to your seat. No lines are permitted outside the restrooms. Thank you for your understanding and cooperation." The tension was thick enough to cut with a knife—but knives were missing from the dining trays when lunch was served.

The flight over the Atlantic was uneventful until a couple of hours before our arrival in Detroit. The pilot came on the intercom and told us we had just flown into American airspace. The passengers erupted. Clapping and sobbing filled the cabin, but this was only a preview of the response when we touched down and taxied off the runway. To this day, tears form when I recall the pilot's announcement, even as I write it now: "We've landed at Detroit Metropolitan Airport, in the United States of America. Welcome home."

Dedicated to the people who experienced the horrors of September 11 firsthand, and to those who lost a loved one in that horrific tragedy.

Recluse

The doorbell rings, breaking my concentration and further souring my mood. "Today's Tuesday, not Friday," I mutter under my breath. "Who's on my porch?"

Deliveries aren't unusual here in the boonies, about ninety miles south of the Canadian border, but they're not commonplace either. No one ventures out here to chat. The internet hasn't invaded this remote rural county yet, so people contact me by snail mail or on my landline. It's better this way.

My veteran's disability and Social Security checks only go so far, and to make ends meet, I've been polishing a story into something a desperate periodical will publish. Pushing the papers aside, I rise and start down the stairs. The doorbell chimes again, and I yell, "I'm coming!" At the bottom of the stairs, after an impatient double doorbell, I shout, "I said I'm coming already!"

A peek through the reinforced door's peephole reveals two grim-faced men with bulges under their overcoats, shuffling their feet in the sub-zero temperature. Their attention focuses when I unlock the two deadbolts and open the door. The storm door remains locked, giving me a veneer of protection; I can talk to strangers without opening it.

"Whad'ya want?"

"US Marshals. We want to talk with you."

Crap. Not again. I thought I was done with that, with the shooting.

"Show me some ID."

Calloused hands mash two badges against the weathered plexiglass window. The cards could be counterfeit. How would I know—I've never seen a US Marshal badge. After all, fake military credentials could be bought on any Saigon street corner in the '60s. The grainy photos match their faces, but I'm not inviting them inside, where it'd be too easy for them to jump me. The nearest potential witness lives a half mile away and knows better than to poke around here.

After unlocking the storm door latch, I step onto the wooden plank porch, while remaining in view of the security camera.

"Mister Vincent Jackson?" the older marshal asks.

"Yes, that's me."

The younger man shoves a document at my chest, sending me a step backward.

"You've been served."

They tramp down the porch stairs, rubbing and blowing on their pink fingers. The marshals plow through a foot of snow back to their black SUV. The car speeds away, kicking up clods of frozen dirt on the two-lane road back to town.

After securing both doors, I zig-zag around the kitchen table and its solitary chair to reach the refrigerator. Pausing before grabbing a cold beer, I remind myself there's no reason to leave here. Fruits and vegetables form neat rows in the field between my faded brown house and the woods. Scraggly sunflowers on withered winter stalks separate carrots from empty tomato cages. A chicken coop, surrounded by barbed wire to keep the coyotes out, sits on the other side of the clapboard building. My freezer is filled with venison, some of which I harvested legally during deer hunting season. The Walmart Supercenter, sixteen miles away, carries canned goods, booze, cigarettes, and foodstuffs I can't provide for myself, and they deliver my grocery orders on Fridays.

My life has been far from exemplary, but I've never done anything to deserve a visit from US Marshals. At least I don't think I have, except for the assault charge when a guy insulted another Vietnam vet, so I beat the shit out of him. Besides, the beer-fueled bar fight happened years ago when I was a ticking time-bomb. This must be about the shooting four months ago. A man died.

Settling into the scruffy sofa, I light a cigarette pulled from a half-empty pack and tear open the manila envelope. "Blah, blah, blah," it reads, and then, "You are ordered to appear at the Federal District Court in Billings at 10:00 a.m. on January 27, 2026. A Grand Jury will question you about the events of September 1, 2025. Your attorney may accompany you, but not inside the Grand Jury room." My attorney? I can barely pay my heating bill this winter, let alone a lawyer.

My eyes return to the date. Last year's Labor Day. "Not this again." Most everything after the shooting remains a blur, and it's a struggle to remember what

I told the cops before they took off the handcuffs. My involvement in the killing had been clarified—it's old news. Blue smoke rings materialize from my pursed lips.

When was the last time I ventured outside this one-stop-sign town, other than that horrific day at Fred's wheat farm, twelve miles away, across the state line? And why did I go? A close by coyote howls, reminding me this isolated farming community protects me from humanity and vice-versa.

But, no, I had to go to the Motown music festival. Publicity promoted this event as another Woodstock. The all-day celebration of classic Motown groups would kick off with some tribute bands before the headliner— The Detroit Derbies—took the stage. Jimmy Germail and The Detroit Derbies. Their music swept the country in the early '60s and they played in all the memorable venues: The Fox Theater in Detroit, the Chicago Theater, and Madison Square Garden in New York City. They even played in Tiger Stadium. Four platinum albums certified their success.

Fifty years after I first heard them, I still enjoyed listening to The Detroit Derbies on CD and wanted to see and hear them perform in person again. My favorite hometown band, their signature black-and-white derby hats and tuxedos fascinated my impressionable teenage self. The quartet's infectious beat and falsetto harmony reminded me of better times.

Before my family abandoned their lunatic son. When I had a steady girlfriend. Listening to the music brings me back to the '60s when we laughed and sang and danced all night before making love. Before Vietnam fucked me up.

*   *   *

After checking into a cheap motel on the outskirts of Billings—all that I can afford on the Federal Court's miserly travel reimbursement—I roam the streets. A single car glides to a halt at a red light, allowing me to cross the street. Most people out tonight are solo, and one of them hits me up for money.

The gaunt panhandler says he needs it for rent, but the guy's glazed eyes and offensive stink tell me all I need to know. Disheveled hair, missing teeth, and one unlaced sneaker paint a complete picture. His pusher is probably nearby, watching for a payoff, and the absent shoelace would be a tourniquet so he could shoot up some heroin. Been there, done that. Better luck with the next sucker.

The movie theater lets out, and people disperse, talking about CGI and the surround sound score. Many hurry to their cars, others to an all-night diner, and some stragglers enter The Tree Haus. Not a bad idea. I follow them, if only to get out of the late January cold.

The blinking neon light inside competes with thick clouds of cigarette smoke. Fur-lined hunting caps and blaze orange vests hang on a row of deer antlers to the right of the door. A burly bartender wipes a glass while listening to a drunk guy in bib overalls and a red flannel shirt complain about Generation Z. A cracked vinyl stool at the end of the acrylic counter lets me put some distance between me and the other people at the bar. The barkeep pivots to face me, makes eye contact, and asks, "What'll ya have?"

"A beer."

"We got Bud, Bud Lite, Miller, Miller Lite, Hamm's, Stroh's—"

"Hamm's."

A frosted mug, filled to the brim with "the beer refreshing", arrives on a cardboard coaster, white foam sliding over the thick rim. Printing appears when I lift the stein off the coaster, "Beer today, gone tomorrow." Sure hope I'm gone tomorrow. Concerns about testifying elbow their way to the front of my mind. How long will it take? What will they ask me? What do they want from me?

In the cramped interrogation room at the police station, the cops had asked me why I went to the concert and why I was onstage. But my answers tomorrow better line up with my story after the killing, or I might not escape this time. What did I tell them before? A normal person in this spot would have trouble remembering. How am I, a recovering junkie with PTSD, supposed to remember what I said when the cops took turns shouting at me?

I tap the bottom of the pack of cigarettes until one stands out. My nerves calm after the smoke from the second cigarette finishes swirling in my lungs. My mind has replayed the instant I heard the gunfire hundreds of times. I had pulled out my Glock and pointed it downward and to my right, but in the direction of Jimmy Germail, where he lay bleeding out. The only man in the world who made me smile after I got back from Nam, and I watched him die.

The brutal image of me on the raised platform, Glock in hand, aimed at a dying man, splashed across newspapers and TV for days. It sure looked like I killed

Jimmy, standing next to his body, my Glock pointed at him. After that, people in town avoided me even more than usual. Letters to the Editor called for my execution. Everybody thought I did it, including the police, at least at first.

A long exhale puffs out my cheeks. I'll have to relive this goddamn nightmare tomorrow, moment by moment.

Just what I needed, another reminder of men in my squad dying to defend Khe Sahn. Night after night after night, shadowy figures scaled the barbed wire after intense mortar attacks. I manned a .50-caliber Browning on the perimeter and dropped too many of them to count. The surviving North Vietnamese soldiers shot off the head of the guy feeding the .50-cal belt on the seventh night. And the guy who took his place—the same night—before my squad retreated.

An occasional heroin dose gave me temporary relief after those brutal attacks. I monitored my doses so I wouldn't get addicted and timed them so it wouldn't reduce my effectiveness. My habit increased after I arrived back in the States in 1970, and gruesome nightmares tormented me after the Marines discharged me. My random psychotic episodes became more frequent, and that's when my family disowned me.

Pawning my Bronze Star in 1975 to finance a hit convinced me I had hit rock bottom. After I came down, I checked myself into an inpatient VA drug program. Sporadic sleep was the best I could manage during that time, and then only with Thorazine. Years later, the VA docs switched me to prazosin. Alcohol was forbidden while on these drugs, but I alternated between sleeping pills and booze for days at a time.

I missed my dad's funeral while I was in rehab, and I think my mom died during this period, too. Their other son, my little brother, drowned in Lake St. Clair in 1962—years before I went to Vietnam—about a quarter mile from shore. He went under before I reached him, and I would have joined him, except lifeguards dragged me into their boat when they got to the scene.

The VA shrink recommended I find somewhere I could avoid loud, unexpected noises and to keep taking the pills. In 1984, I found a house in a remote setting, with a roof needing repair almost as much as I did. I started living a routine life—at least routine for me— but sleep began eluding me the last five months. Again.

The walls feel like they're starting to close in on me, like before I got clean. "Breathe deep through your nose, from your belly," my drug counselor had taught me after

I arrived stateside. "Think of holding hands with your girlfriend." Doesn't help.

I finish the draft and walk back to my monotone tan motel room.

*   *   *

The clock radio alarm goes off, though nightmares kept me half-awake all night. Thoughts swirl through my mind while I sit on the side of the bed. Don't lose your temper. Count to three before answering each question. Keep your responses short—yes or no are best. It's OK to say you can't remember if it's true. Keep telling yourself you're innocent. Keep your head up.

A hot shower refreshes me, and I read a leftover newspaper while I tuck into a fast-food breakfast across the street. After the last forkful of half-cooked hash browns, I lean back in the booth while I finish my coffee and light a cigarette. The middle-aged waitress frowns at me and points to a NO SMOKING sign above my booth, so I smile back at her and leave. Back in the dingy room, I slide my Glock between the mattress and box spring. I hang a Do Not Disturb tag on the doorknob on my way out.

After disabling the alarm on my 2009 pickup and checking the back seat, I open the primer-orange driver's door and climb in. I toss the newspaper—I didn't finish reading it before the waitress kicked me out—onto the gray duct tape holding the torn bench seat material together. A quick glance at the mirrors tells me no one is lurking nearby, so I turn the key. The engine responds with a roar and a puff of blue exhaust, reminding me to replace the muffler or at least cover the rusted hole with sheet metal again. Damn.

I pull out of my parking spot and turn left onto the street after signaling, but only when there's no traffic. A cop could arrest me for driving with an expired license—the nearest Secretary of State office is over an hour's drive away from my house. Keeping the Grand Jury waiting for any reason, especially an arrest, would not go over well.

Twenty minutes later, I maneuver my truck into a parking space and shuffle into the Federal Building. My shoulders sag—I didn't get much shut-eye last night—and the greasy breakfast doesn't sit well. A magnetometer affirms the decision to leave my piece behind. Up two floors and down the institutional hall, a molded plastic chair outside the assigned room wobbles when I sit down. The hands on the Hammond clock overlap at 9:48.

A pale, frail man leaves the Grand Jury room at 10:54, glances at me, and takes a step back. A combover suggests his hair color once matched his baggy brown suit. The spooky figure peers at me through bifocals set in a round metal frame, like the kind John Lennon wore the night he was shot and killed. A blink, and he scurries away, his rubber soles squishing on the tile floor.

At 11:22, a man in a navy-blue suit and striped tie emerges from the room and says my name as a question. After I nod yes, he motions to follow him inside.

Worn paths on the room's linoleum floor reflect decades of foot traffic. Fluorescent bulbs flicker. Soot covers some of the mismatched tiles in the suspended ceiling while the newer ones shine. The man—he must be the District Attorney—points to a raised box where I sit on a hard wooden chair. An oversized pull-down movie screen stands a few feet away, on my left. A slide carousel sits on a card table a few feet in front of it, its fan whirring.

About twenty people in padded folding chairs, arranged in a semi-circle, stare at me. Most appear to be in their forties or fifties, a few are younger, and the rest are older. One lady sitting in the front row—she's about my age—has thinning gray hair and thick glasses perched under a frowning forehead. Four of the men are wearing suits and ties, the rest sport casual shirts and pants. No blue jeans or overalls. Ordinary people. Were any of them in The Tree Haus last night?

After I'm sworn in and advised of my limited rights, we go through the preliminaries of name, date of birth, address, etc. The District Attorney cuts an imposing figure, over six feet tall with no flabby bulges under his suit jacket. He begins to pace back and forth in front of me.

"Where were you on the afternoon of September 1, 2025?"

"On Fred Green's farm."

"Why were you there?"

"To see a music show."

The District Attorney takes the lens cap off the slide carousel and uses a laser pointer to identify me on the screen. "Are you in this photograph?"

Glancing to my left, the terrifying image looms larger than life. The picture shows me standing over a dying black man, my Glock pointed toward him, amid chaos on the bandstand and in the hysterical audience. His derby hat lay askew next to him, and blood soaked his tuxedo. Band members have dropped their instruments, and some are rushing toward Jimmy while others stand in shock. People in the audience are pointing toward the stage. But are they pointing at Jimmy or at me?

A shudder runs through me, and I take a deep breath to prepare myself, just like the Marines taught me to do before going into combat. All the grand jurors stare at me, frowning.

Stop. Don't smile. Breathe naturally. I exhale, but not too much.

"Yes."

Questions and answers come rat-a-tat in his rich baritone voice. "Why did you carry a gun to a concert?"

"I always carry my gun."

"What specific gun do you own?"

"Glock 19."

"Is it the same gun that's in the photograph?"

"Yes."

"Do you have it with you now?"

Be careful. Answer the question he asked. Keep it short. Where it is now doesn't matter.

"No."

Immediately, "What's the capacity of your Glock 19 magazine?"

"Fifteen rounds." Slow down! Don't let the DA set the tempo.

"How many rounds were in the magazine after the shooting?"

I pause. "Thirteen."

"Did you fire your gun on September 1, 2025?" asks the District Attorney.

Where is he going? A slow breath. "Yes."

The room goes silent as the jurors, especially the old lady, glare at me. That's a yes-or-no question, but I can't let it go without an explanation. "Earlier that morning, I took two quick shots at a coyote poking around my chicken coop. Missed 'em." Damn! Too quick with my alibi for the missing ammo. Sounds like I rehearsed it, like I was trying to cover something up.

The District Attorney's cadence quickens, as does his pacing, back and forth, in front of me.

"Where were you in 1968?"

"Khe Sahn, Vietnam."

Another quick question.

"Why were you in Khe Sahn?"

"That's where the 26th US Marine Brigade was stationed."

The DA stops in front of me, pauses, and stares into my eyes through oversized black framed glasses.

"What happened while you were in Khe Sahn?"

"The North Vietnamese Army beat our brains in for six months."

He folds his arms and lowers his voice.

"Where were you sent after Khe Sahn?"

"To the VA Hospital. The doc said I had post-Vietnam syndrome. Now they call it PTSD."

The District Attorney slows the pace. "Were you charged with Felony Assault and Battery in 1979?"

"Yes, but it got reduced to a misdemeanor."

"What was the race of the man you assaulted?"

"He was black."

The District Attorney runs a hand through his slick-backed hair, then raises both hands, palms up.

"Why were you onstage with an African American band?"

"I was singing and dancing in the front row, havin' a ball, like it was the '60s again. Wearing their signature derby hats and tuxedos, The Detroit Derbies entertained me just like the old days. During their break, I yelled at Jimmy Germail, the lead singer, 'I saw you in 1966 at the Driftwood Lounge in Detroit, the night before I got shipped to Nam.' Jimmy grinned and waved me up."

"Why did you aim your gun at the victim?"

Given an opportunity to elaborate, I break my rule about short answers. "My gun isn't aimed; it's pointed. The Marines taught me to point my weapon down and to the right when I draw it, as a safety precaution, instead of pointing it into a crowd." For the first time, I'm giving my side of the story. The pulsating blood in my veins slows a bit after another deep breath.

"Is part of your safety training to not watch where you're pointing your gun?"

"My weapon is pointing where it's supposed to, down and to the right." He's not going to get away with mischaracterizing basic firearm safety. The jurors' eyes follow my finger, directing their attention to the enlarged image. "In the picture, my head is turned away from Jimmy. I'm looking up, over, and past the crowd."

"Why are you looking up?"

"I'm trying to find where the shots came from."

"Why would you know where the shots came from?"

"From being shot at while in Viet Nam."

"Did you see a shooter?"

"No."

"Did you see anything in the direction you were looking?"

"The only thing that stood out was a nearby mesa."

The District Attorney straightens his suit jacket and turns his round face toward me.

"What caliber is your Glock?"

"Nine mil. And that's another thing; Jimmy was killed by—"

The District Attorney stops mid-step and spins around to face the jurors.

"Stop! The witness has no direct knowledge of the murder weapon or its caliber. Jurors will disregard the witness's attempt to identify the purported weapon and caliber. The jury will rely solely on the coroner's testimony earlier today on this issue."

Why did he ask me about my Glock and the old assault and battery charge? He's painting me as the shooter, but he knew an assault rifle killed the aging African American icon. Ballistics proved I didn't shoot him! The local paper had printed the forensic evidence report right before Thanksgiving, showing Jimmy died from two .223 slugs fired from an assault rifle.

"No further questions. You may step down."

What! That's it? All the way to Billings for this? Confused, I stumble out of the box and exit to my right with my head held high. Relief flows from my head to my feet. The same cheap chair in the hallway beckons me, and I collapse in it, shaking and wobbling.

Think! Why did they subpoena me? What did the DA want from me? Why did he ask about my Glock, its magazine, and where it was pointed? He set me up as a potential suspect, with means and opportunity. The questions about PTSD painted me as a crazy man. Was the question about beating the black guy in the bar years ago supposed to establish a motive? Nothing makes sense.

The door to the Grand Jury room remains ajar, and I tip-toe to it, standing behind the door jamb.

The District Attorney says, "Ladies and gentlemen of the jury, you have just heard Mr. Jackson's testimony about his role in Mr. Germail's murder. Mr. Jackson is a decorated war hero who, unfortunately, suffered terribly from what he experienced during his tour of duty in Vietnam. The Marines taught him how to handle a firearm in combat, something he remembers to this day at age seventy-eight."

"No shit, Sherlock."

"No doubt many of you read the newspaper accounts the day after the shooting and saw that photograph of Mr. Jackson on stage. I'm asking you to forget all that you read and to focus on Mr. Jackson's explanations for his actions on September 1, 2025. The witness testified that—"

My cough interrupts the DA's summary, and rushing footsteps squeak on the tile floor just before the door slams shut.

I return to my rented room and note the Do Not Disturb hangtag still dangling from the doorknob. Inside, I lift the mattress, retrieve my Glock, sniff the barrel, and check the clip. It hasn't been fired. Lying down doesn't help me figure out why I got a subpoena. Two cigarettes don't either.

Now it's early evening and too late for the seven-hour drive home. Driving at night isn't possible anymore. Truck headlights become the spotlights we used in Khe Sahn and trigger memories of the nighttime attacks. Six months. The siege at Khe Sahn lasted six months. Every night was the same—mortar shelling followed by infantry attacks. Khe Sahn is mammoth—the perimeter was almost ten miles around—we couldn't guard every foot of it. The North Vietnamese Army took advantage of the air base's size.

Back at the cheerless tavern, I take the same worn stool.

"What'll ya have?"

"Hamm's."

The suds come with a cardboard coaster that says, "Don't worry, beer happy," provoking a subdued chuckle. Hunched forward, my elbows rest on the acrylic counter and my chin rests on the top of the triangle formed by my arms. I spent all my energy in the grand jury room, but I can't rest until I figure this out.

"Tough day today?"

A nod.

"Wanna talk about it?"

I shake my head and count three glum patrons scattered among the tables, nursing their drinks. Two bored women are dancing out of rhythm to an '80s rock classic blasting from the Wurlitzer. A couple groping each other in a back booth is trying, and failing, to be discreet. After wiping a wine glass, the barkeep checks for smudges in the light, then returns to the cash register.

I yank a pack of smokes from my shirt pocket. A friction match scritches, and its reddish flame is pulled toward the cigarette when I inhale. I sit, smoke, sip, and stew.

"Another," I say, lifting the mug.

More Hamm's arrives and takes its place on the damp coaster.

"Can I get somethin' to eat?" Breakfast was a long time ago and it sucked.

"Burger and home fries?"

"Sure."

"Whad'ya want on it?"

"Grilled onions, lettuce, and tomato."

Sliced potatoes protest the moment they hit the heated oil. The barman, now a short-order cook, slaps a patty on the grill and covers the sizzling burger with a dented tin lid. Chopped onions dance in melted butter next to the split bun, and the sweet smell of grilled onions starts my mouth watering. A few minutes later, it all comes together in front of me, along with a caddy containing ketchup, mustard, relish, and mayonnaise.

Does the greasy bar food satisfy me because I'm starving, or was it the intense afternoon? Either way, the red plastic basket is empty minutes later, except for the checkerboard wax paper and plastic silverware.

My hand rises. "One more."

The bartender clears the basket and condiment tray and replaces the empty glass with a full one, eyeing me askance. My return scowl tells him to back off. Yeah, it's a little early, and I'm pounding 'em back pretty good, but I've had a long, hard day. Last night's prazosin tablets gave me what little sleep I had, but its now-familiar interaction with alcohol leaves me buzzed and sluggish.

Two customers walk in, jingling the bell on the doorframe, and the bartender greets his regulars by name. Now is a good time to go, so I drain the last of the Hamm's, stick two twenties under the coaster, and disappear out the door. After weaving my way back to the motel, I hang the Do Not Disturb tag on the doorknob. The combination of drugs and booze knocks me out soon after my head hits the pillow, though hallucinations rotate among today, Vietnam, and that bloody Labor Day.

* * *

Waking by sunlight beats an alarm every time. The day starts with a steaming shower and another lousy breakfast across the street. I pick up another discarded newspaper and take pleasure in the familiar rustle of newsprint. An article on page three grabs my attention: "Grand Jury leak on Motown Festival killing."

"A Grand Juror spoke on condition of anonymity about yesterday's proceedings. The initial suspect, Mr.

Jackson of Medora, North Dakota, confirmed the location of the fatal shots. He was dancing with The Detroit Dandies when Mr. Germail was shot, and Mr. Jackson's Marine training and experience in Vietnam took over. He drew his Glock and instinctively turned toward the sound of the gunfire. His testimony corroborated that of the coroner, who used the slight downward geometry of the bullet wounds to indicate an elevated shooter. He testified the killer might have been on a mesa over two hundred yards away. Mr. Jackson confirmed that direction. A State Police spokesperson said an arrest in the case is imminent."

That's it! The DA called me "the witness" when I tried to tell the grand jury what the murder weapon was. And I overheard him call me "the witness" before he closed the door to the Grand Jury room. Grand juries don't hear testimony from suspects, only from prosecution witnesses.

The District Attorney had a huge problem—the photograph had caused many people to prejudge that I was guilty, which newspapers the next day strongly implied. Destroying the perception created by the photo had to precede other questioning, hence the questions about my Glock, why I had it with me, and the two missing rounds.

And that's why the DA stopped me, when I started to tell the grand jury Jimmy was killed by two .223 slugs. He worked hard to clear their suspicions of me from what they read in the newspaper. The DA didn't want my testimony on the direction of the fatal slugs discredited because of hearsay about their caliber.

What was I telling the grand jury right before he excused me? . . . "In the picture, my head is turned away from him. I'm looking up, over, and past the crowd, trying to find where the shots came from." Is that what he needed from me, the shooter's location, because I had the best view and a trained military reaction?

Ain't that somethin'? Things are never this complicated back home, and home is where I'm heading. My refuge lies seven hours away, but there won't be any truck headlights in the afternoon. Prazosin promises better sleep tonight.

* * *

The truck's tires pop the loose gravel when I turn into my driveway. A sudden movement near the chicken coop attracts my attention, so I get out of the truck but don't close the door. Sliding my Glock from its holster,

I flick the safety off and grasping it with both hands, I point it at the ground by my right side.

I creep toward the chicken coop where all hell is breaking loose. Hens are squawking and feathers are flying everywhere. They're running in circles and their wings are beating. Taking a breath and exhaling as the Marines taught me, I raise the Glock to eye level. One decisive stride gets me around the corner of the hen-house, where I swivel my outstretched arms.

Pop! Pop! Pop! Copper shell casings eject up and to the right, arcing through the air.

The mottled grey coyote lies on its side, twitching its legs, but only for a couple of seconds.

Life's a lot simpler here. The bad guys don't shoot back.

Maggie

My phone rang late in the afternoon, showing my wife's number. Maureen rarely called me at work. "I'm at the vet's office, with Maggie. . . . Her heart is failing." A pause, then, "Bruce says she won't live through the day. Do you want to be with her . . . when they put her down?"

The commute took less than the usual fifty-five minutes. Memories of Maggie splashing into Williams Lake and lunging at a bobbing tennis ball elicited crimped lips, not a smile. "Please hang on, please hang on," I chanted through sniffles until I pulled into the parking lot.

Maggie was an unexpected present at my fortieth birthday celebration, and my life changed the first time she sprang into my lap and licked my face. Becoming each other's best friend, we swam together and played hide-and-seek in the house and in overgrown fields. Mundane errands provided excuses for us to flaunt our friendship around town. While I was teaching her obedience skills masquerading as games, she was teaching me undying devotion. Maggie's last lesson, after ten inseparable years, would be a heartrending reminder of the frailty of life.

Maureen and Maggie were waiting for me when I rushed into the institutional lobby. Faded photographs of leaping dogs, playful cats, and adoring owners plastered the peeling beige walls. Only it wasn't the Maggie I was familiar with—no tail wag, no perked head when she spotted me. Taking ragged breaths, she sat at Maureen's feet, motionless, her black nose dry and head drooping. How should we spend our last minutes together?

The two of us trudged outside for our final game of fetch, her favorite pastime. A well-chewed tennis ball rolled a few feet in front of her, and she gazed at me as if to say, "I can't." Maggie's most cherished toy remained in the muddy weeds, abandoned, when we went back inside.

Bruce, our family veterinarian leaned in. "Let us know when you're ready. You can be with her, or

Melanie"—cocking his head toward the technician next to him—"will do it in the lab." A bright pink syringe hung lifelessly from her hand.

How do you say goodbye? My arms engulfed her, and I kissed her mottled gray muzzle. A deep inhale struggled to capture her smell forever. "Good girl," I said, petting her auburn flank with trembling hands. "Down." Maggie laid down with a slight groan, obedient to the end. My steadfast companion stared into my eyes. Did she know?

Melanie waited for me to finish my farewell. I vowed not to let Maggie see me cry. Gritting my teeth, I bobbed my head twice without looking up. Melanie knelt beside me, hypodermic in hand, and deftly inserted the needle into Maggie's foreleg. She pushed the plunger. A distant voice soon said, "She's gone," but I kept stroking her lifeless side. I gently removed Maggie's collar.

I don't remember how I got back home. No one ran out the door to lick my face.

Hurricane Helene

"SO HOW BAD WAS IT?" asked a Michigan friend a few days ago, "Hurricane Helene, how bad was it?"

I told him we lived in downtown Asheville, which didn't bear the brunt of the September 28th storm, and our condo building escaped without any damage. "We were inconvenienced, not like people who lost everything, including over 100 who died in western North Carolina." Power, running water, text, phone, and internet all failed throughout the city that dreadful day, which meant I couldn't contact anyone to tell them we were safe. Back in Michigan, our adult children witnessed the devastation in and around Asheville on TV and social media, wondering if we were dead or alive.

On day two, Nancy and I stood in line for three hours before entering a grocery store, where the empty shelves reminded us of COVID. We took cold "submarine showers" using cans of soda, a washcloth, and soap, finishing with dry shampoo. Our lights flickered back to life that night, allowing us to savor our first hot meal since the storm. On the third day, a national grocery chain donated an entire semi tractor-trailer loaded with cases of six one-gallon bottles of water to anyone who asked. We gave thanks for a significant upgrade from soda for our submarine showers. Text and phone service returned on the fourth day, providing contact with the outside world, and we heard sighs of relief from several states away.

Every day I hauled a five-gallon bucket from the creek across the street and carried the 42 pounds 210 steps to our apartment. The precious water filled both our toilet tanks, and we each limited ourselves to one flush a day until running water, and the internet, were restored three weeks later. We jumped at the opportunity for a hot shower, ran the dishwasher, and washed a mountain of clothes for the first time in almost a month. A "boil water advisory" compelled us to use bottled water for cooking, drinking, and brushing our teeth. But like I told my friend, these were inconveniences. We were fortunate.

About 80% of Asheville's beloved River Arts District, home to restaurants, shops, and an eclectic movie theater, was submerged under more than 20 feet of water. Over 300 artists lost their studios, supplies, and their stockpiled inventory of paintings, sculptures, and crafts. Residents of Biltmore Village, also south of downtown, reacted when floodwaters breached their first floor, forcing them upstairs. The water rose with them, and families fled to their attics. The water soon followed them, and they exited onto the roof through gabled windows, all in less than 30 horrifying minutes.

Pause to think how terrified you would have been. How much higher would the water rise? Where could you go? Imagine thinking, "Is this how my family will die?" Mercifully, the torrent stopped at the gutters. Their homes were a total loss, but they survived, rescued by the Cajun Navy in their bass boats.

Chinook helicopters began flying overhead almost every hour, landing at the closed Asheville Airport, where the National Guard offloaded food and water into trucks for delivery to distribution centers. One of Nancy's childhood friends was airlifted by a cable into a military helicopter, as were other people living in remote, inaccessible locations.

Hurricane Helene mud damage

Several towns nestled in idyllic valleys next to placid rivers were swamped by cataclysmic 27-foot walls of water rushing down the mountains. Half of downtown Chimney Rock just disappeared, and the mayor said rebuilding it would take at least a year. Not even debris remained in some towns, like Swannanoa, a bedroom community east of Asheville. Beacon Village, a middle-class development in Swannanoa, boasted 77 houses before the hurricane. Most of them were swept away, inundated with mud, or suffered irreversible water damage and mold, leaving 11 habitable homes. A Facebook video showed a house floating down the Swannanoa River, being sliced in two as it passed by a concrete piling, a remnant of a washed-away bridge.

Interstate expressways north, west, and east of Asheville collapsed—the only way to leave town was south. Seven weeks later, eastbound I-40 opened, and people found, and shared, alternate northern and western routes out of the city traveling on two-lane county roads.

But amidst this devastation, people started helping people. Nancy found an NPR station which transformed itself into an aid clearinghouse, matching needs with assistance. The host put one man on the air, saying a huge tree fell across his driveway and he couldn't get out. Another caller said he had a chainsaw, and the radio station's back-room telephone volunteers matched them up. A homebound woman called the station needing insulin and a way to keep it chilled. They connected her with a man who picked up a fresh supply at her pharmacy and gave it to her in a new name-brand cooler full of ice. A "wilderness experience" company converted their mules from transporting tourists up and down mountains to packing supplies for stranded families. During the first three weeks, the station broadcast too many heart-warming stories to mention.

Some people in rural areas who had propane generators could draw water from their wells. Kelly, a counselor at a nearby food pantry, put two 95-gallon trash bins in her pickup truck and filled them with water. She and her husband drove into a subdivision and started knocking on doors, holding a pair of five-gallon buckets. "Hello," she'd say, "I'm Kelly and I'm here to flush your toilets."

Workmen in fluorescent vests appeared like a swarm of bees, clearing wreckage and repairing infrastructure. Republican and Democratic politicians all praised the speed and magnitude of relief provided by an alphabet soup of federal, state, local, and charitable agencies.

A line of women appeared at a rural staging area for out-of-state electrical linemen, who worked twelve-hour shifts without access to running water or clean clothing. Each woman stepped to the head of the line and took the dirty, smelly shirt, socks, overalls, and underwear a workman wore that day. The ladies returned the next day with laundered work clothes. A Facebook meme, "The best linemen are not in the NFL," went viral.

Area churches provided ad hoc shelter and relief to anyone, regardless of religion. A James Beard Award-winning restaurant supplied 1,000 free meals a day, as did several other eateries. The World Central Kitchen, led by Jose Andres, fed 23,000 displaced people in the first three days after they fashioned a base of operations. They remain here, providing free meals, almost three months later. A big-box home improvement chain purchased and donated 3,000 Thanksgiving turkeys, complemented by an array of side dishes.

A nearby neighborhood held a massive grill party, cooking meat before it turned bad. Residents emptied their refrigerators and fed neighbors they had never met. This subdivision endured extensive destruction from trees falling on homes and cars, and downed power lines blocked many streets, but their community spirit triumphed. Clearing the mud and debris lasted over a week, and home repairs continued for two months. Ubiquitous piles of sawn tree trunks and cut branches still line their neighborhood streets, squeezing traffic to one lane. One city block close to our condo continues to draw its electricity from an insulated power line laying across Starnes Avenue, due to a lack of poles.

Normalcy is sporadically returning in select areas. The Health Department lifted the boil water advisory on November 20. Most restaurants in the central business district have reopened, though with reduced menus and reduced staff, but some are closed permanently.

A glass-blowing shop in the River Arts District is open and holding classes. Another artist is selling decks of playing cards created from 54 of her ruined paintings as a fundraiser for affected artists. Retail stores on the higher side of Biltmore Village are open, as are some pubs. The Biltmore Estate is resuming its classic holiday decorations and tours. Traffic congestion has returned, but dark clouds hover over the tourist industry—one of Asheville's largest employers. The Paris of the South was devastated, but the spirit of its people ensures it will survive.

Asheville Strong.

First published in Contingencies, American Academy of Actuaries, Jan/Feb 2025.

Hitchhiking to Hingning

An ancient gong shares a sizable grassy courtyard with a Chinese pagoda on the Maryknoll campus in Ossining, north of New York City, with both structures painted Mandarin Red. One by one, the members of my outgoing class marched up to the bell on a sunny June morning in 1949 and rang it with the ritual mallet. Then it was my turn, and I strode to the suspended bell, gave it an emphatic WHACK, and rejoined the privileged party of missioners. The surrounding sisters applauded after the resonant BONG, and I burst with pride. Mother General Mary Joseph gave us our assignments afterward, and I learned I was going to China!

The departure ceremony had ended, we had our assignments, and eighteen young women regressed to adolescence—the elation reminded me of my First Holy

Maryknoll departure gong

Communion. I screamed, "Today is the best day of my life!" My emotions merged with those of the other missioners, spilling out like a river overflowing a dam.

The ceremony was bittersweet. None of my family were here to celebrate this joyous occasion with me. My brothers and sisters couldn't leave their homes for a week to come to Ossining, and Mom couldn't travel alone. I was jealous of the other sisters whose relatives clustered around them—a sin of envy I confessed at the following week's Chapter of Faults. I'd seen my family only once in the seven years since I entered Maryknoll—when Dad died.

A new stage of my life began that day—more like I'd been reborn. Chicago and Ossining were the only places I'd ever lived, and I'd never been on a train other than the "L" outlining Chicago's downtown Loop.

Two months later, Mother General handed me more money than I'd seen in years, assuring me I'd need it for a boat trip across the Pacific Ocean. "Leapin' lizards," as Little Orphan Annie would say.

Southern Pacific Railway poster

For four days in August's brutal heat and humidity, I wore full Maryknoll regalia: black habit and lisle stockings, "granny shoes," and a black cowl buttoned to a stiff, two-ply white cardboard cap. A small fortune lay buried deep in my habit's inside pocket. Transferring trains in Chicago's mammoth Union Station from the Manhattan Limited to the City of San Francisco was a daunting challenge, but I did it.

The endless clickety-clack of rail travel lulled me to sleep every night while sitting upright in the coach car. The menu in the dining car never changed, and Cheerios with berries reminded me of home. However, my love of tomato soup and a grilled cheese sandwich for lunch was put to the test by the fourth day. Money was an issue, so drinking water instead of milk saved me a nickel at each meal. A succession of cities paraded before me in the observation car, followed by small towns separated by farms, and at long last, the snowcapped Rocky Mountains. The panorama of America broke the monotony of reading the Bible and memorizing more sections of the Catechism.

The protracted journey finished at San Francisco's Transbay Terminal, where I joined a lengthy taxi line. After a brief wait, I climbed into the crinkled back seat of a Yellow Cab and asked the beefy driver to take me to the ocean liner wharfs. "I'm going to China!"

"Not by ship, you ain't," said the cab driver, over his shoulder. "The longshoremen are on strike, so no boats have entered or left the harbor for weeks. They ain't even negotiating."

"What? How will I get to China?" *Was I asking him or me?* Two thousand miles from Ossining, I stared out the car window at this strange city and blinked away the moisture prickling in my eyes. The cabbie's blue eyes, set in a kind face, peered at me in his rearview mirror. I began to sweat. *There's only enough money for a second-class cabin on some ship. Could anyone—*

"Sister? . . . Are you okay?"

Thoughts whirled in my head. *Settle down, Sister Marion. Think!* There had to be a Catholic convent somewhere in this city. It wouldn't be Maryknoll, because our sisters are all either overseas or in Ossining, but I was sure the nuns would let me in, whatever order they were. *Would they let me stay until—*

"Sister? Do you want to try the airport?"

"Sure . . . I suppose." My limited cash could pay for a cheap boat ride, but wouldn't cover an extravagance like airfare. Still, I didn't have another travel option.

Forty minutes later, the cab pulled up in front of the "Departures" sign at San Francisco International Airport.

"No charge, Sister. You'll need all the money you got for an airline ticket. Besides, now I've done my good deed for the day."

For what good it did, I was at an airport, but not even halfway to China. *Now how to get the rest of the way to Hingning? What should I do? Oh well, 'In for a dime, in for a dollar,' as Dad used to say.*

The hectic terminal, humming with busy travelers toting bulky luggage, swallowed me whole. Hungry, and lugging two heavy suitcases myself, I found the crowded cafeteria and chose a table near the front. The waitress, a pleasant woman in her forties, brought me a paper menu for a placemat. "Good afternoon, Sister. What'cha havin'?"

The flimsy menu listed familiar food, and I chose the cheapest offering. "An egg salad sandwich and a glass of water, please." I marveled that an egg salad sandwich cost forty cents just because I was in a busy airport. *Shame on this place, charging seven cents for a soda. Thank the Lord the cabbie didn't charge me, so I could afford something to eat.*

I needed to watch what I spent so I'd have enough money when the strike ended, whenever that might be. *Should I go back to Ossining? Probably not, because Mother General would send me back here when this thing's over, and that would cost Maryknoll two more cross-country—*

Laughing and poking each other, two genial men wearing bomber jackets with Air Force insignia took the table next to me, mumbling about weather reports. After ordering two Cokes, the younger one eyed me up and down and furrowed his brows. "Not many nuns pass through here. Where ya goin'?"

"China—at least I'm trying to get to China," I said between offering grace for my lunch and taking a bite of it.

"China? That's a long way to go, especially for a nun traveling alone." The statement oozed skepticism, all but demanding an explanation.

"I was supposed to get on a slow boat to China, but the dockworkers are on strike. No ships are going anywhere." My hands rose off the table, palms up. "So I came here."

"So . . . you're stranded?"

"I gotta find out if I have enough cash for an airline ticket to China—Canton—but I'm doubtful." I twisted the wedding ring on my right ring finger while giving them my best smile. "If not, . . . then yes, I'm stranded."

The younger pilot leaned in, concerned, and lowered his voice. "What's your plan?"

"I just got here, so, no, I don't have a plan yet. You don't happen to be going to China, are you?"

"Naw, we're carrying cargo to Japan, with some stops in between for fuel."

Across the Pacific Ocean! *Dear Lord, is this part of Your plan?* An idea began to take shape.

"Do you carry people?"

"Military passengers, top brass, and folks like that."

Lowering my head and blotting my lips with the napkin hid my disappointment. *Is there anything wrong with a nun being friendly to strangers?* Inching my chair closer, a manufactured smile appeared when I raised my head. "How many passengers do you usually have?" I silently prayed, *Good Shepherd, please coax these men to take Your lost lamb across the ocean.*

"Sometimes one or two, sometimes five or six. One time, we had eleven. In a few minutes, we'll meet a guy who's coming with us."

"Only one passenger this time?"

"Yep."

You can lead a horse to water . . . Keep them talking, Sister Marion.

"Is he a serviceman?"

"Sorta."

Head down, I remained silent—like in Ossining, not the easiest thing for me to do. A deep sigh followed another bite of my runny sandwich and a sip of water. *Forty cents for this? Too much mayonnaise, no celery, and could use more eggs, but at least it was toasted, like Mom's.*

The younger airman elbowed his partner's arm, and they conferred, whispering. The older veteran frowned, shrugged his shoulders, and muttered, "Sure."

"Sister, I'm Dave, and this is Pete. We can take you as far as Manila. That's most of the way to China."

"I'm Sister Marion Cordis. May God bless you!"

I looked up, thinking, *Thank you, Jesus.*

The pilots stood and Dave tossed a generous quarter on his table; I left forty-five cents for my skimpy sandwich. Giving thanks for lunch had to wait, though I was ambivalent whether it deserved the recognition. Each Air Force veteran took one of my battered suitcases when we got up from our chairs. A man with a ramrod-straight posture and ill-fitting civilian clothes confronted our odd-looking trio as were leaving the cafeteria.

"Who's she? And why is she here?" demanded the irritated and unnamed stranger.

"Sister Marion Cordis. She's coming with us to Manila," Dave said.

"Who approved this?"

"Me," snapped Pete. "I'm the pilot." The rumpled civilian opened his mouth, then shut it with a stern frown.

The four of us departed the terminal and marched in an edgy single-file line—Pete, me, Dave, and Grumpy. An imposing silver aircraft with four huge engines and larger propellers awaited us. The massive machine boasted an impressive five-pointed white star in a blue circle on its side. I'd never seen an airplane this close up, let alone ride in one. A quiet voice broke the silence. "Can this make it all the way to Manila?"

"It's a Douglas C-54 Skymaster, the military version of the civilian DC-4," said Pete. "This bird's range is four thousand miles, so we'll make stopovers for fuel along the way—in Pearl Harbor, Guam, and Manila."

C-54 Skymaster

"How high does it go?" What concerned me was how far we'd fall if we crashed.

"Cruising altitude is ten thousand feet, where the temperature 'll be around twenty-five degrees, so bundle up. The air up there 'll be thin, but we won't need oxygen masks, only ear protection." He jerked his thumb at the plane. "Get in."

As ordered, I climbed up three corrugated iron steps to the side hatch, hiked up my habit with one hand and grabbed an interior handle with the other. After hoisting myself up, Airman Dave, who was already inside, directed me toward a row of metal seats bolted to the side of the fuselage.

"Comfy?" he asked with a goofy grin.

Grumpy sat opposite me, intriguing me, so I asked him, "Why are you going to Japan?"

In a flash, Dave swapped his playful demeanor for a deadpan expression. "We got cargo bound for Japan, and you don't need to know anything else. Now buckle up, Buttercup, we're takin' off soon."

The propellers came to life, one after another, sputtering and smoking until the blades got up to speed, forming four hazy disks. Pete taxied to the runway and paused. Dave wasn't kidding—the noise was deafening, so I put on my earphones.

With a jerk, the airplane leapt forward and somehow the tremendous racket increased as we picked up speed. But we were still earthbound and chewing up the remaining runway at an alarming rate. My fingers grabbed the edge of my seat, and I spied Grumpy staring at me with an annoying grin. The plane overcame gravity as we passed twenty feet over waves lapping at riprap rocks, pushing me down in my seat as it climbed. I glimpsed ships in the Pacific beneath us, distracting me from Grumpy and the incessant roar of the engines and propellers.

About two hours out of San Francisco, dark clouds engulfed us and the Skymaster contended with an immense storm. Gusts of wind shoved the plane from side to side while hail pelted its aluminum skin, sounding like a string of firecrackers on the Fourth of July. A bolt of lightning struck the right wing, the lights flickered, and the heavy Skymaster shuddered.

"What's happening?" I shrieked, but my hysterical words were lost in the roar of the thunder, the engines, and the propellers. The airship plummeted what must have been two hundred feet, but my stomach didn't fall quite so far. "Are we crashing?"

Grumpy shook his head, scowling, and continued reading his sheaf of papers. The Skymaster swooped up a hundred feet in an instant, pressing me down in my seat while jerking me around, reuniting me with my stomach. My saliva bore a metallic tang.

Lord God, I spent my entire life preparing to be a Maryknoll missionary. Was this where my life would end? My trust was in the Lord, but I thought back to the Pentecost Sunday a few months earlier to distract me from my imminent doom.

Mother General motioned to me after the morning Mass ended and held out a thin white envelope. "Here is your assignment. Use the next—"

Another pocket of turbulent air rattled Grumpy and me and whatever war matériel was riding with us. My queasy stomach cramped, while runny mayonnaise rolled over my tongue.

I unfolded the letter. "China! I'm going to China under the direction of Bishop Ford!"

I tried to focus on the Maryknoll cofounder's directive to visit at least one family every day. Mother General extended his mandate, instructing us to call on every household within a *pulu*—walking distance from the mission—once a month.

Mother General repeated Bishop Ford's charge after we all rang the ceremonial gong, ordering us to live the Apostle Luke's description of early Christianity: "From house to house, they kept proclaiming that Jesus is the Messiah."

My insides shifted higher, a sudden chill gripped me, and perspiration formed on my forehead. Muscle spasms began deep in my belly. Unnatural sounds escaped my mouth. I clenched my teeth, unwilling to give in to my body. Another abrupt drop in altitude and I puked over my lap and onto my shoes.

Ashamed, I snuck a peek at Grumpy, who was smirking. The handkerchief in my inside pocket failed to remove all the vomit from my habit, and it became too filthy to wipe off my shoes. And my hands stunk. Several stifled sobs later, a bright red overtook my ashen face, further humiliating me. Grumpy put down his reading and stared at me. My head lowered in shame. I couldn't help myself. *What was I supposed to do?*

The violent storm subsided, and the pilots executed a smooth landing in Hawaii. While the aircraft gulped fuel, I tried to rinse myself off in the terminal's cramped kitchen. Dave ambled up next to me and put his hand on my shoulder. My head turned away, too embarrassed to meet his eyes.

"Happens to all of us. I've done it; Pete's done it too." My feeble smile did nothing to remove the stench from my clothing.

"Ginger ale works better than water. Here's a couple of bottles and some rags. Shake the bottle to get it fizzing."

Uncapping and jiggling the first one, I discovered the soda-soaked rag worked wonders on the remaining vomit and the odor. My habit was somewhat clean and still stunk, but much less than before. The second bottle removed most of the mess from my shoes, though pieces of partially digested egg salad still hid among the laces and eyelets.

"Thanks, Dave. You're a lifesaver. I couldn't stand myself the rest of the way."

"You're welcome. I wouldn't 've been able to stand you either." A chuckle, then, "C'mon, I'll buy you a cuppa tea to settle your stomach."

* * *

The transit to Guam was blessedly calm, and the airmen relaxed when we reach cruising altitude. Dave removed his headset, rose from his seat, and sauntered back to me, grabbing the overhead rail for balance.

"Quite a downpour between Frisco and Pearl, wasn't it, Sister?"

"I prayed to God the whole time—except when I was throwing up."

"We'll take all the help we can get. The forecast for this leg says we'll have smooth air the rest of the way." Stretching his arms, he gave an exaggerated yawn, plopped down next to me, and fastened his seat belt. The surprised expression on my face betrayed my concern.

"I need a break after the thunderstorm," he said with a mischievous wink. "Go up to the cockpit and sit in my seat."

"But I can't fly an airplane!"

"I'm a little rusty on that myself. Besides, nothing can go wrong with God as our copilot. Did you see the movie? Dennis Morgan acted like a real pilot." The aviator snickered at his reference to the popular 1945 motion picture highlighting the Flying Tigers.

"Pete and me flew with the Tigers in China. In 1941, we were volunteers but officially members of the Chinese Air Force and wore Chinese insignia. We battled Japanese Zero fighters twelve days after Pearl Harbor." A soft whistle accompanied a head shake. "The Japs were damned good—oops, sorry Sister—darned good flyers, and their machines were better'n ours. Pete's unit held its own against 'em in several dogfights. We were lucky to get out alive."

My hand landed on Dave's forearm. "God really was your copilot."

"Funny, isn't it?" Dave said. "America was an ally of China against Japan in the war, and now we're carryin' cargo to Japan for our soldiers. They're gonna battle Mao and the Chinese communists sooner or later."

For the next hour, Airman Pete taught me to fly. An unsisterlike snort escaped when I remembered Dad's admonition: "Women can't do certain jobs, like being a policeman. Women won the right to vote, but that doesn't give them the right to do men's work."

Peering upward through the forest of dials, levers, and switches, I called out, "Look, Dad, I'm at the controls of an airplane, two miles above the Pacific Ocean."

This small achievement reminded me of Little Orphan Annie, a nationwide radio sensation that entertained our family before and during the Great Depression. The Baumwolle family would gather in the parlor after dinner to listen to a Philco Model 512 with its matching mahogany speaker broadcast her adventures. Each program traced one day in young Annie's life as she confronted corrupt politicians, gangsters, and shady institutions, protecting frightened and defenseless people from overpowering villains.

The strong female lead character, sponsored by Ovaltine, fascinated me at the impressionable age of nine. Piloting an airplane might not be as rewarding as foiling a crooked politician or a heartless banker, but I found it just as meaningful. The catchy jingle opened every radio installment, and now it streamed out of my mouth.

Who's the little chatterbox?
The one with pretty auburn locks?
Who can it be?
It's Little Orphan Annie.
. . .
Now, wouldn't it be worth the while
If you could be
Like Little Orphan Annie . . .

Pete turned in his seat, glanced back at Dave, and shrugged his shoulders.

* * *

Fifty-two hours after departing San Francisco, we landed in the Philippines, and my saviors continued to Japan after refueling. The Maryknoll Sisters in their Manila convent greeted me with open arms, at least until they got a whiff of me. Keeping their distance, they escorted me to my room, where I changed into a fresh habit and scrubbed my shoes. They reinforced my chopstick lessons daily, interspersed among weeks of trying to obtain transportation to Canton.

The convent's Mother Superior told me the crews on boats leaving Manila were much different than the

American crews that would have left San Francisco. "Here, they're little better than pirates," she said, shaking her head. "A lone woman on a ship leaving Manila might not still be on board when it anchors in Canton. For you, flying is the safest way to get to China."

A few days after celebrating American Thanksgiving by eating sesame chicken and bok Choy with chopsticks, Mother Superior arranged a meeting with a seedy, unkempt man. She told me to ignore his appearance, and that he could get me to Canton ". . . if I kept an open mind." After some haggling, we used much of my remaining money to pay this intermediary for a seat, a bribe really, on another military cargo plane. This one was as noisy as the other one, but the sky was clear and sunny.

As the Fairchild C-119 circled above the rudimentary Canton runway, I stared down at hundreds of bright green islands scattered across a broad network of sparkling waterways. What a beautiful country! A soft bump signaled the pilot's expert landing, and the plane taxied to the primitive passenger terminal.

I did it. I made it to China!

Acknowledgements

The stanza from the "Little Orphan Annie Theme Song" was taken from *Little Orphan Annie Theme Song* by Gus Kahn, published on September 11, 1928 and initially aired on WGN (Chicago radio) in 1930.

Hurricane Helene was first published in *Contingencies*, American Academy of Actuaries, Jan/Feb 2025.

The following images were found in the public domain via Wikimedia Commons.

Original attributions are:

- GIs on ship – Ministry of Information Photo Division Photographer
- Fort Sheridan – Historic American Building Survey/National Park Service
- City of San Francisco poster – Southern Pacific Railway poster
- C-54 Skymaster – USAAF

The following images were found via Wikimedia Commons with appropriate licenses for commercial use and requested attribution:

- Chicago Water Tower – Amaury Laporte, CC BY 2.0
- Jemaa el-Fna – Luc Viator.JPG, CC BY-SA 3.0
- Hurricane Helene damage – NCDOT communications, CC BY 2.0

The remaining images were taken from the author's collection of personal photographs.

Peter Selgin designed the front and back covers. His artist's intuition created an eye-catching collage of 1950-era images. Thank you, Peter.

The pleasing appearance of titles, text, headers, and photos is due to Steve Straus's interior formatting. Thank you, Steve, especially for your patience.

Kim Wiley was my no-nonsense developmental editor for *Faith and Fury: An American Nun in Mao's China* and four of the short stories. Lois Wolfe Markham provided actionable guidance for several short stories, submitted over the course of her writing classes. Shelby

Newsom's expert eye caught innumerable typos, grammar mistakes, and other errors. Thank you, Kim, Lois, and Shelby. You improved these stories.

Kellie Scott prodded me twice. She informed me that a single sentence in *Faith and Fury: An American Nun in Mao's China* about Sister Marion's journey from San Francisco to Hingning deserved an entire chapter. *Hitchhiking to Hingning* was the result. As a beta reader, Kellie encouraged me to disclose painful memories in *The Visit*. Thank you, Kellie. Both your suggestions were correct.

Debbie Gurriere has been a faithful beta reader for several projects, including this one. Debbie always amazes me with her unique suggestions for improving my work. Thank you, Debbie, and I eagerly await your next appearance on stage.

The final recognition of people responsible for this book goes to my very patient and understanding wife, Nancy. She was my most trusted, and oftentimes blunt, beta reader.

I claim sole responsibility for all the errors appearing in this book.